About The Author

Maureen, although a mother of three and grandmother of seven, maintains that she is really just a kid at heart and so it is easy for her to enter into, and create, a child's world! Her writing is motivated by a desire to entertain young people while at the same time injecting into her stories elements of philosophy to promote thought and reflection. Maureen's teaching career, spanning many years, has included the teaching of philosophy, English, history and teaching children with special needs. She holds two masters' degrees and a doctorate in education.

The Sorcerer's Gifts

Maureen McDermott

The Sorcerer's Gifts

Nightingale Book

NIGHTINGALE PAPERBACK

© Copyright 2024
Maureen McDermott

The right of Maureen McDermott to be identified as author of
this work has been asserted by her in accordance with the
Copyright, Designs and Patents Act 1988.

All Rights Reserved

No reproduction, copy or transmission of this publication
may be made without written permission.
No paragraph of this publication may be reproduced,
copied or transmitted save with the written permission of the
publisher, or in accordance with the provisions
of the Copyright Act 1956 (as amended).

Any person who commits any unauthorised act in relation to
this publication may be liable to criminal
prosecution and civil claims for damages.

A CIP catalogue record for this title is
available from the British Library.

ISBN 978 1 83875 692 5

This is a work of fiction. Names, characters, businesses, places, events and
incidents are either the product of the author's imagination or used in a
fictitious manner. Any resemblance to actual persons, living or dead, or
actual events is purely coincidental.

Nightingale Books is an imprint of
Pegasus Elliot Mackenzie Publishers Ltd.
www.pegasuspublishers.com

First Published in 2024

Nightingale Books
Sheraton House Castle Park
Cambridge England

Printed & Bound in Great Britain

Dedicated to my seven roguish and wonderful grandchildren who allow me to share their lives.

Contents

Section One

Garth's Story
The Crafting of Courage

A *Boy* and a *River*

*O*nce upon a time, in a country that was shiny green in summer and white and crystal in winter, lived a strong and brave boy called Garth. The boy lived in a small willow and mud cabin with his grandparents by a river's edge. Garth had come to live with his grandparents when he was only a few months old, just before the time when his parents had died at the hands of the powerful and dark master who ruled the land.

Now the boy's grandparents were old and frail and very poor. When the river froze over in winter and they could not fish, or when their small vegetable garden was robbed of its harvest, the small family often went hungry. When Garth reached the age of twelve, he was at last tall and strong enough to help improve the income of his poor struggling grandparents by poling a barge across the wide expanse of the river which flowed past their door. You see, travellers were happy to pay for this service as they were frightened to use the bridge further upstream where a troll sometimes took up residence under the ancient stone arch. People were particularly upset and afraid of the loud sobbing-like noises made by the troll which caused even the stone bridge to tremble. It was agreed among the locals that in many ways the deep utterances made by the troll were even more frightening than his awful appearance!

Garth wondered about the troll, and as he ferried customers across the river, he sometimes had the feeling that the creature's gaze was upon him and that his every move was being watched. The deep troubled cries of the troll disturbed him. He wondered if the creature might be especially calling to him, and he was tempted to go closer to the bridge in order to find out if this was the case. Due to the wariness of trolls and their ways, he always kept a reasonable distance between his small craft and the bridge.

In spite of his growing strength, ferrying a barge across the wide expanse of the river was hard work, but the lad was proud at the end of the day to hand over to his grandparents the pennies that he had earned. The seasons of winter and spring, however, did not allow the boy to work on the river. In winter the river was frozen with a thin layer of dangerous ice (travellers were then forced to use the bridge in spite of their fear of the troll) and in springtime, the river current was swift and dangerous because of melted snow which had flowed into it further upstream in the high country. Garth and his grandparents would, at these times, watch reluctant travellers, full of trepidation, go past their cabin towards the stone bridge where they feared the troll might be in residence. Although the boy loved the wild nature of winter and the beauty of emerging life in spring, he fretted because he could not, at these times, contribute any money to ease the hard lot of his grandparents' life.

He dearly loved the elderly couple and they in turn were very kind to the lad, and in spite of their poverty, did their best to make his life pleasant and good. They were surprisingly well-read, and were keen to teach their grandson about the discoveries and ideas of great thinkers of the past. In the evenings, particularly in winter, the three would sit by the fire and the old people would share with Garth what they had read and learned over the years. They would, at times, read to him from a small library of worn leather-bound books which they said they had managed to save from other times.

The years passed with quiet regularity, and Garth took for granted his life and home with his grandparents. One evening, not long after his fourteenth birthday, on completion of the day's chores he sat on the riverbank to watch the setting sun. The colours of the sunset were particularly beautiful, and the calmness of the approaching night combined to lull the boy into a reflective mood. He fell into wondering about what sort of people his dead parents had been and about the manner of their deaths. He resolved to ask his grandparents about them, so one evening after the family had finished a simple but satisfying supper, Garth thought it an appropriate time to bring up the subject of his dead parents. When he did, however, the old couple were strangely quiet and reluctant to talk to him about the matter. Their reluctance to talk only spiked his curiosity further, and from rarely thinking about his parents, Garth came to wonder about them all the time.

A *Dark Monarch's Tribute*

Once a year, roughly at the approach of winter, soldiers would turn up in the district. They rode from cabin to cabin banging on doors and demanding the tribute, which was imposed by the king. The tax was large and each year Garth's grandparents, like all of their neighbours, found it difficult to pay.

One day when Garth was nearly fifteen years old, the elderly couple set out on a journey to the market to trade for much needed supplies to get them through the winter. The pair pulled a small handcart loaded with vegetables that they had harvested in the last weeks of summer. Along with the vegetables they also had a bundle of fish that they had caught in the river over previous months and had dried, smoked and wrapped up in bark ready for transporting to market. After loading the cart, Garth chose not to accompany his grandparents to market but set to the task of chopping and stacking wood for the cold months ahead. There had been a certain cheery nature to their goodbyes as the three realised that for once what they had to trade at the town market would provide better than usual provisions for their winter stores.

Garth was happy with his progress and whistled as he stacked the cut wood. The whistle died on his lips, however, as he looked up at the sound of approaching galloping horses. The horses and their riders drew to a halt outside the cabin and signalled to Garth, who was some distance away, to come quickly. There were no greetings exchanged between the boy and the soldiers but the sergeant who led the troop aggressively demanded the annual tribute payable to the king.

The boy was desperate to satisfy the soldiers and see them on their way as he knew they were impatient and capable of causing serious damage to property if kept waiting. He rushed inside and found the box that was under the old couple's bed where all important family papers were kept. He found the money at the bottom of the box wrapped up in an old rag, but as he pulled it out something caught his eye: a piece of parchment folded over and tied with a frayed white ribbon. On the outside of the parchment Garth saw his own name written in large faded letters.

Garth slammed the lid of the box shut, pushed it under the bed and ran outside to give the soldiers the money. The sergeant who had been waiting impatiently snatched the rag with its contents, counted out the money and roughly threw the rag to the ground. Two minutes later the king's tax collectors had mounted their horses and were away into the distance to the next cabin.

The lad returned to his labour of chopping and stacking the wood but now with little pleasure in his work. The power and rudeness of the soldiers reminded Garth of his precarious existence. No matter how hard his family — and indeed the people of the country — tried to make a basic living and enjoy the small pleasures attached to living an honest and good life, there was always in the background the spectra of the monarch who ruled them with such a cruel and heavy hand. Resentment over the status quo was something that was rarely talked about in a family and certainly never among neighbours for fear of being betrayed to the authorities. Alongside Garth's resentment over the unfairness and ruthlessness of the king, however, ran another thought that wove itself in and out of his thinking all day: the letter in the box — the letter that had *his* name on it!

Just as he finished stacking the last log, he arrived at the conclusion that as the letter was addressed to him he was in his rights to take it out and read it. Yet another line of reasoning persisted: the box and its contents were sacred to an adult world — to the world of his grandparents — and before this day he had never opened it. By sunset, however, he could resist no longer and he returned to the box.

A *L*etter from *L*ong *A*go

*H*e noticed that his hands were trembling as he raised the lid. He hesitated before picking up the letter because he had an overwhelming sense that once read, the letter would change his life for ever. The parchment was yellow with age and fragile to the touch. He untied the frayed ribbon and opened the letter very carefully while all the time his heart was pounding so hard he thought he might faint. He was immediately surprised to find inside the folded parchment a large and beautiful pendant.

It was round in shape. The outside border was made of silver and there were words engraved on its lower half. The pendant showed signs of much handling and because of this the words at its base were difficult to read. The inner circle was made of gold and at the very centre there was a large green gemstone. Garth supposed that it was an emerald and he was astounded that anything so valuable could be in the possession of his grandparents. The thought also lightly crossed his mind that since the ornament was inside a letter addressed to him, it might also belong to him. After fingering it for a few reflective moments the boy, anxious to read the contents of the letter, slipped the pendant into a pocket of his tunic. Then, sitting on the beaten earth floor of the cabin, he turned his attention to the letter and slowly read the following:

Our dearest son,

Your father and I will be dead many years before you read this letter, but know that we loved you dearly. Our time in this world is short as we can only hold out against the forces of the king for perhaps another hour. I am entrusting this letter to a faithful servant who will stay hidden in a secret cavity in the wall until the king's soldiers have done their murderous work and departed.

I hope with all my heart that this letter will eventually reach my parents who I have entrusted with your care. They will, in time, pass this letter on to you so that you might attempt to rescue your sister and destroy the dark master who rules Balkonia. The hope of this letter one day reaching you is all that your father and I have left.

At the sight of the word sister, Garth was thunderstruck. 'Sister, sister,' he said over and over again. 'I have — or have had — a sister!' Then he went back to the letter written by his mother many years before.

The story of our family is a strange one. Many generations ago we were gifted with unusual powers by an old and wise sorcerer. These powers were given with the expectation that they would be used in the service of good. In every seventh generation, the first-born child — if a girl — is born with an extraordinary power, far beyond other family members. The sorcerer set out that this powerful force would emerge when a family member drank the water of the Crystal Stream high up in the mountains near the Monastery of The Three Peaks.

Your sister is a seventh generation first-born, but is only now three years old. The king is aware of her dormant power, and because of this he and his soldiers have taken her from the holy monks whom we charged with her protection when these troubled times began. The king will, in time (when he has won your sister's support) take her to drink at the Crystal Spring. Alas! We die with the sad knowledge that we are powerless to stop him!

It is known by all that the king, through his cruelty and greed, is losing his power over the people of Balkonia who wish to overthrow him — and in time they may. But should he gain your sister Rosamund's powerful assistance, his grip on this land could never be overthrown.

My son, you too have some of the strange force that lies in your sister but it will never be as strong in you as it is in her — it is not your destiny. Nevertheless, for the sake of this sad land you must go up into the mountains and drink the Crystal Spring water and then use

*whatever gift you are given to overcome the king — even
if this means…*

Here the letter stopped.

Just as Garth finished reading what his mother had
written to him so many years before, his grandparents
entered the cabin. The elderly couple were stunned
when they saw the letter in Garth's hands but Garth
hesitated before saying, 'I had to give the soldiers the
king's money or they would have burnt our cabin to the
ground.' He hesitated again before continuing. 'I saw
this letter… and after all, it is addressed to me!'

There was a long silence and then his voice lost its
apologetic tone and he said assertively, 'Why haven't I
been given this letter?'

The boy's grandparents looked confused and sad
and then, after a long pause, the old man answered in a
hushed tone.

'We haven't been honest with you in this matter
because of the danger involved, and because we have
already lost so much to the actions of this evil king! We
lost your parents,' (and here the old man's voice
faltered), 'we have lost your sister and… we can't bear
the thought of losing you!'

Garth, still in a confused and shocked state, further
demanded in a loud and angry voice, 'I have a right to
know everything. I have been charged by my parents to
do what I can. I have a duty to try to set things right!'

Crossing a Bridge

*H*is grandfather placed his hand on Garth's shoulder and led him to the rustic table, which was at the centre of their cabin. Here, they waited in silence while his grandmother prepared special food that had been bought at the town market, and which had been intended to be a rare treat for them all.

They ate in silence. Garth did not even notice what his grandmother had prepared. After supper was over and the bowls and utensils were removed from the table Garth lifted his head, and looking at both his grandparents said, 'I am sorry for the rude and ungrateful way I spoke to you. No matter what your reasons are for withholding the letter, you are the kindest and best of grandparents. So please forgive me.'

His grandmother leant across the table and took his hand.

'You are the best of grandchildren, and while we would have kept you longer with us we know that it is time for you to hear about your history and to set out on your parents' given quest.'

By the light of a spluttering candle the three talked long into the night. Garth listened intently as his grandparents unfolded the long sacred history of his family. From time to time he interrupted to ask them something, and in response to one question about where they had originally come from his grandmother replied:

'We were not always poor as you see us now. We were part of a group of families who worked together to care for and govern Balkonia. I believe that we were just and good administrators and we did our best to rule wisely.' Here the old lady looked at her husband who nodded in agreement.

Garth learnt that way back in their history his family had been honoured by an old sorcerer who had granted them power to protect their ancient land from evil forces that had been threatening it at that time.

'The power is still there,' said his grandfather. 'Yes, we have it too but it is not very strong in us… and the evil is great.' Here he looked at his wife. 'The loss of family exhausted my will and that of your grandmother long ago, and we made up our minds that our mission was to care for you and keep you safe. We also knew that we had to give you the letter in time so that you could set out on the almost impossible quest that is your lot.'

The symbol of their family's destiny, they told the boy, was the pendant that had been given to them by the sorcerer as a symbol of their inherent power. Garth produced the pendant from the pocket in his tunic and looked at it intently, trying to make out the message at its base. An hour or so past midnight they at last went to bed with the knowledge that Garth was determined to set out that very day on a quest to free his country from the rule of the dark king (and, if possible, to bring back his lost sister).

At dawn after a scant breakfast of hot oatmeal, Garth embraced his grandparents and slung his bedroll and a bag full of provisions over his shoulder. His grandmother asked him for the pendant and placed it around his neck, and as she did so she whispered the words: 'Courage is crafted in adversity.'

Garth was surprised by the formality of these farewell words from his grandmother, but apart from looking at her quizzically he did not question her about them. With a final reflective look at the elderly couple and a slow wave of his hand, Garth ventured out into the chill early morning air.

The boy walked briskly along the bank of his beloved river. He breathed in the comforting smell of the smoke coming from the neighbouring cabins and he listened with pleasure to the whispering winds drifting down from the mountain range which lay to the northwest. In spite of all these pleasant sensations, his mind was also burdened with a nagging anxiety about all the information that his grandparents had given him over the hours of the previous evening. The few hours' sleep between going to bed and rising had also been troubled, yet he was still full of hope that he would eventually set things right. Adding to these anxieties and expectations was another troublesome thought eating away at the back of his mind. He knew that the dreaded bridge was just ahead and that he would have to cross it in order to set out for a more direct route to the mountains.

Holding his breath in nervous anticipation, Garth stepped onto the bridge. Immediately a troll burst out from under the arch! He was small in stature and his features were awful! His arms were long and thick with knotted muscles. His mouth was wide, his teeth were pointed and sharp and his body was covered in thick brown fur. Garth was transfixed with fear, but he was a brave and thinking boy and he calmed himself down so as to evaluate the situation in which he found himself.

Is he baring his teeth so as to attack me? Or could he possibly be smiling at me? he wondered. The troll spoke first, in a deep and troubled tone, and words rushed out in quick succession.

'We meet at last, boy! I have often called to you and you have never answered me. I like you. I listen to you sing your river songs and… and I watch you work hard on the river. I have wanted to help you — we could work together. I am so much stronger than you, and with my help your life would be so much easier! I am so lonely! We could be friends. Have you not heard me call to you?' The troll's voice lost its deep edge and became almost pleading.

Garth was amazed. He did not answer at once but thought back to the many times he had heard the troll's strange and haunting calls. With slow deliberation, he said, 'Troll, I am sorry that I have not answered your calls and made an effort to meet you. I will be your friend — if I return from my quest — and we will work together on our beautiful river. Before we can do that I have an important task to accomplish: I must rescue a sister from the clutches of the evil ruler of our land; a sister who may not want to be rescued. And then,' he continued slowly and purposely, 'I have to destroy the king himself so that the people of our country, as in times gone by, may once again live without fear.' For a moment or two the enormity of what he had to achieve overcame Garth and he stared at the troll, unable to speak further.

'That is an awesome and difficult task,' whispered the troll in a low voice and he too paused, unable to find words. Then in a rush he said, 'The dark ruler of this land is no friend of trolls either… or anyone else for that matter. I would be happy to come with you. I am strong and I could help you in so many ways'. Here, he turned briefly to face the mountains in the far distance.

'I see that you are setting out for the mountains. I know the mountains well, for when I am not here as keeper of this bridge I am up in the high country exploring every pathway and looking into every nook and cranny.' At that point there was a childlike quality of expectancy that spread over the frightful features of the fierce keeper of the bridge as he waited for the boy's answer.

Garth, for the first time, saw past the scary features of the troll and in their place he saw a being who was strong, heroic and lonely. He hesitated to say no to someone who could be a good and reliable travelling companion, but after a short hesitation Garth shook his head.

'My quest is dangerous and I am not certain that I will survive it. No, my new and strong friend, I must face this quest alone. It would be wrong of me to involve you.'

Garth swung his bag of provisions from his shoulder and said to the troll, 'I have set out early and I have not had much for breakfast. Will you join me? May I share with you some provisions that my grandmother has prepared?' The troll nodded his agreement. They retreated to the small fire that the bridge keeper had made under the arch and shared a meal together.

They ate in silence and when they had finished Garth re-packed his sack. Standing, he offered his hand in friendship to the troll. The creature looked into the eyes of Garth and after a moment's hesitation took the hand offered to him into his own strong grasp. From the two massive eyes in the centre of his furry face, the troll then watched Garth set out for the mountains.

A *Not-So-Friendly Meeting!*

*H*e walked in a north-westerly direction towards the mountain range, which retained a snow cap at its highest point from the previous winter. In the early morning autumn light the mountains in the distance looked startlingly beautiful.

'Somewhere — somewhere up there in those majestic heights is a fresh water stream', he murmured aloud. 'Let me at least find the Crystal Spring so that whatever power I have can emerge, and after that I can seek out and deal with the evil king. And my sister? Ah! What will happen there?' he wondered.

For three days he walked towards the beautiful snow-capped range. At times, he wished that he and his grandparents had not been so poor and that he could have lessened the time and distance by riding a horse. As night descended, he would gather wood, light a small campfire and prepare his evening meal that for the most part consisted of bread, cheese and vegetables which he boiled into a warm comforting soup.

It was the third night of his journey. The sky was ablaze with stars and Garth, overcome with awe at the beauty of the night sky, couldn't sleep. He took the pendant from around his neck, and by the light of the fire he looked at it closely and at length for the first time. He gasped when he at last deciphered the inscription at the base of the pendant. He read the words which his grandmother had used as her farewell to him three days before: courage is crafted in adversity. The boy fingered the ornament for some time before replacing it around his neck.

I must be prepared for anything, was his last thought before at last falling into a troubled sleep.

Garth's encounters with people on his journey were few. Once, he met a family of five on the move. They looked poor and everything they owned was in a small cart which the father had harnessed to his thin but strong shoulders. There was hardly any greetings between them. The mother gathered her children to her and hurried by while the father gave Garth a hesitant nod. On another occasion the boy came across two men struggling to fix the broken axle on their cart. He immediately took the sack from his shoulder and prepared to help them, but they scowled at him and refused his offer of help. These episodes only highlighted for the boy the depth of suspicion that abounded in his country, and he was saddened by it.

While he had little communication with people, Garth fed his soul with natural things that surrounded him. He felt keenly the subtle beauty of the songs of birds that had not flown to warmer areas for the winter but instead would endure through the cold winter months, singing their songs on winter wood. The geometric beauty of geese flying south for the winter filled him with awe, and he was transfixed by flashes of burnished gold when foxes broke through the undergrowth and ran onto open ground. From time to time, however, the boy felt uneasy. Was he being followed? He would pause in his walking to look behind but there was never anyone there. Garth eventually put his suspicion down to anxiety about what might lay ahead and he made a conscious effort to resist the urge to look behind.

The first snow heralding the approach of winter came in the early hours of the afternoon of the fourth day as he reached the foothills of the mountain range. The area was heavily wooded with conifers and deciduous trees still sporting some remaining autumn foliage. The area was also marked by many rocky clefts and outcrops. The boy trudged along for some considerable distance looking for somewhere to begin his climb. At last he found what he had been searching for: a track leading up through the trees and rocks.

He climbed steadily for two hours, going up considerable distances, but then the path would digress and slant downwards and he would lose some of the height that he had gained. The late autumn sun was setting low in the sky and the snow was getting heavier, but still he kept on telling himself that he would stop and make camp soon. He was focused on finding kindling as he went along, when suddenly the path was blocked by a herd of long-horned cattle being driven along by an old man wearing a black, enveloping cape and carrying a long staff.

The man's face was brown and leathery and his general appearance was one of weathered toughness. Garth thought he saw an expression that was cruel and cunning, and he became anxious to move past the man and his herd of cattle to continue on his way up the mountain. Still, Garth's fears were allayed when the old man spoke first in a not unfriendly voice.

'Where are you going, lad, so late on this chilly autumn day?'

'Good afternoon to you, sir. I am on my way up the mountain to search for a watercourse named the Crystal Mountain Stream. Do you know if I am heading in its general direction?' asked Garth. 'I believe that the stream is somewhere near the Monastery of the Three Peaks, but I imagine that I have a great deal more of a distance to go.' The boy waited for the man to reply.

The old man looked intensely at Garth before saying, 'Why do you seek to find this stream?'

Garth noted that much of the friendliness had disappeared from the man's voice. His original suspicion returned, so he simply replied, 'I seek to find the spring for private reasons'. Then after a slight pause (and with as much courtesy as he could muster) the boy brushed past the herder and attempted to find a gap through the long-horned cattle.

A knowing and cruel look came over the man's face as he watched Garth. In a voice that was cold and menacing he said, 'I am the king's servant and the guardian of the Crystal Stream. Your appearance and your intention to find the Crystal Stream tells me that you are a member of the Adagio family and that you are my lord — the king's — enemy!'

With that he gave an order to the cattle, and with horns down, they moved towards Garth.

Waiting for an Interrogator

Garth backed away in fear. The animals stopped at the old man's command and the boy found himself with his back to the edge of a deep chasm. In front of him the herd of cattle poised, ready to push him over the edge. One particularly ferocious-looking animal lowered his horned head and slowly edged closer to the boy who became aware that one of his feet was slipping over the crumbly edge.

Garth was full of fear and he pleaded with the old man to save him. There was a sinister smile on the man's face and Garth knew that the herder was playing with the idea of seeing him plummet over the side to his death. After what seemed an eternity the old man — with surprisingly quick movements — made his way through the beasts and pulled Garth to safety. Taking a rope from around his waist, he roughly tied the boy's hands together and fastened the ends of the rope across the horns of a particularly strong animal (the one that had threatened to push Garth over the edge to his death).

In response to a shrill whistle, the animals moved off down a side track, which Garth had not previously noticed, and the boy found himself almost jostled off his feet by the animal to which he was tied. Still suffering from the trauma of near death, the lad found it difficult to keep pace with the cattleman and his animals. When he tripped over some tree roots, he was not given time to rise to his feet and was pulled along over the frozen and rough ground. He was soon bruised and bloodied. After fifteen minutes or so, they turned off onto a narrower pathway where it became necessary for the man to allow Garth to rise to his feet, for the ground was too uneven to drag him further.

The light had almost faded when the herder stopped before the narrow and low entrance to a cave. Here, he produced a knife from underneath his clothes and cut the boy's rope. He roughly indicated to Garth that he should crawl through the entrance and that he would follow behind him.

The inside of the cave was dark, and Garth could only vaguely make out the figure of his captor taking a flint stone and piece of metal from his pocket and striking the flint till he lit some kindling that was stored on a rocky shelf next to a bracketed torch. Successfully lighting the kindling, the man set about attempting to light the brush torch. Seeing his captor so busy, Garth realised it might be his only chance to try to get away. Garth knew that outside the entrance the unfriendly cattle were bunched together in a group, blocking any chance of escape. He reasoned that his only avenue of escape was to run down the tunnel away from the exit.

With his heart beating wildly, and in spite of his stiffness and grazes, the boy managed a fast pace down through the tunnel until, out of range of the light of the torch, he was forced to slacken his progress to a hesitant walk. He desperately felt along the tunnel wall but all the while he could hear the footsteps of the cattleman coming after him. It was a rock in the middle of the cave path, however, that lost him precious time. His sore and tired body landed with a thud on the ground but his face was immersed in freezing water. In a disorientated state, he reacted by gulping for air only to find his mouth fill with icy liquid, which he inadvertently swallowed, dragging himself away from the cave stream, and rising as quickly as he could to his feet, he floundered onwards, only to be confronted by a stone wall that barred any further progress. Seconds later, the old man caught up with him and levelled a knife at Garth's heart.

'Now, lad, I so want to kill you — and I could do it so easily — and if you resist further I will do it! Or you can come with me without a struggle. You choose now!' Looking at the knife, Garth reluctantly nodded his head, indicating that he would co-operate.

By the light of the flaming torch, Garth could see the old man's hand go behind a ledge in the rock face and manoeuvre something. The stone wall slowly ground open and the flickering light of the torch revealed the horrifying sight of barred cells along the length of a mouldy stone corridor.

With the knife poking into his ribs, Garth was edged forward past the cells. Hands reached out between the bars and tried to clutch their clothes, and prisoners pleaded for food and water. Ignoring the prisoners' cries, the old man pushed Garth towards the end of the long corridor where there was a key hanging from a hook on the wall. Unlocking a heavy iron door, the herder pushed Garth into an even filthier, damp mouldy room.

Rats scuffled across the floor and there was an awful stench that made Garth gag. Laughing loudly at the boy's distress the man said, 'Look — look at the walls, boy, and you will see what the future holds for you!' Garth wiped his mouth with the back of his bloodied and bruised hand and looked to where the man pointed.

To his horror he saw bolted to the walls a number of iron rings. Shackled to one of these rings was one poor prisoner who was obviously in a great deal of pain and distress.

'See,' said the cattle herder with an evil laugh. 'That man there has already been visited by an interrogator Tomorrow it will be your turn, boy. Yes indeed, tomorrow it will be your turn,' cackled the cattle herder as he pushed the boy to the earth floor, 'and you will be questioned as to why you wanted to go up the mountain to find the Crystal Stream. You see, I am certain that you are a member of the Adagio family and that you work against the interests of my lord, the king.

Tonight you sleep with the rats and tomorrow you will be questioned and then chained to the wall where you will starve to death!'

Our Friendship Starts from here and now, eh?

Garth was left alone in the darkness of the cave, his hands once again tied behind his back, only this time his feet were also tied. He was very scared and hungry and his body was aching all over. The coldness of the cave system added to his physical distress, yet his mind was clear and one thought occupied it: *I have to escape by morning before an interrogator comes.* He also wondered about who the interrogator might be. He hoped with all his might that the mysterious person would not be his own sister!

He remembered the way the cattle herder had enjoyed the moment when he had forced him to the edge of the precipice, and he thought with disgust the way he had pleaded with him to save his life. He made a mental note that if he ever escaped his present predicament he would never in his life plead for mercy again, no matter what tools of torture the interrogator might use or whatever situation he might find himself in in the future.

Garth worked hard at trying to get out of the ropes that bound his hands together but he only succeeded in chafing them more, and his misery was further increased by spasmodic cramps that wracked his body. Almost in despair, Garth rested his head against the slimy rock face and listened to the low moaning of the prisoner chained to the wall a few metres away.

Out of compassion for the man's suffering, Garth gently said to him, 'I am sorry for your pain and suffering. I wish that I could help you.' The man stopped his moaning and muttered something that the boy, in spite of listening carefully, could not understand.

Just then, Garth saw a light shining underneath the base of the iron door through which he and the cattleman had entered into this dreadful room of torture and death. He heard the heavy weight of the door swing slowly and laboriously open. It took a few seconds for Garth to become accustomed to the light coming from two luminous eyes and to recognise the strong sturdy figure of the troll that he had met on the bridge four days before.

The troll spoke gruffly, but not unkindly, to Garth. 'Well, boy, you have got yourself into a spot of trouble haven't you? Maybe you need my help? Perhaps we do not have to wait until you return to the river for our friendship to start. I think that our friendship should start here and now, eh?'

The boy looked at the troll in amazement and then said, 'So there *was* someone following me all the time — and it was you!'

The troll's response was to set to work on the ropes that bound Garth's hands and feet, and as he struggled with the knots he relayed just how difficult it had been to stay close enough to the old man so as to see what he was doing.

'I followed you both down the tunnel and I watched the cattle herder put his hand behind the ledge and pull a lever to open the stone door. I had to keep my eyes almost shut,' he told Garth, 'so their light would not give my presence away.'

He pulled the last rope from Garth's hands and threw it away with a flourish.

'Now let's get out of here, boy. We haven't got all that much time, you know!'

'Not so fast' said Garth. 'First, we have to unchain this poor man here.' Garth searched among the keys hanging on the wall till he at last found the one that undid the bracketed ring. 'Listen,' said Garth to the man when he had freed him, 'we cannot stay to help you out of the cave, but as we go we will leave the doors open. And good luck to you!'

It took some time for the two to find their way out of the tunnel because as they passed the cells which held the prisoners, they could not ignore their cries for help. They stopped momentarily to throw the bolts on the doors open so that the inmates would also have a chance to escape. At last they reached the narrow opening of the cave that led to the outside world. For a brief

moment Garth stopped and looked into the two massive
eyes of his new friend.

'Thank you,' he said with deep feeling.

A *Good Piece* of *News*

Later that evening, by the warmth of an open fire Garth and the troll cemented their friendship. Garth discovered how practical his new friend was when the troll brought the bag of provisions that he, Garth, had dropped when he had been captured by the cattle herder. These were very welcome to both of them! Garth then told the troll the history of his family — as recently told to him by his grandparents.

'And so I have to drink the water of the Crystal Stream which flows past the Monastery of the Three Peaks. I have to find this stream quickly before we are discovered by the cattle herder or the king's soldiers, or worse, the interrogator,' he said.

Garth drank thirstily from the leather canister that the troll handed to him, and as he drank he confided in his furry companion.

'This is the only drink that I have had in twelve hours, except for the mouthful of water that I gulped when I fell into the stream in the cave.' At these words the troll began a loud and deep satisfying laugh accompanied by a little thumping dance. Garth was surprised!

'Why are you laughing?'

'Oh, you silly human!' said the troll. 'The water you gulped was that of the Crystal Stream which flows through the cave system from further up the mountain. I told you that I knew the mountains well. Don't you know anything?' Garth forgave the troll for his lack of manners because he too was excited about his having already drunk from the magic stream.

'Well, well!' he said, more to himself than to the troll. 'How will I test myself to see if I have any powers?'

They both searched around for something to test a possible new power.

'See if you can make the flames of our fire rise up to the height of that tall tree there,' suggested the troll. Garth looked at the fire and tried to think the flames up, but there was no increase in the intensity of the fire.

'Focus harder,' said the troll. The boy closed his eyes and concentrated with all his might and at the same time slowly lifted his hands in front of him. In spite of his energy and focus, nothing happened.

'Wherein do my powers lie?' he asked his friend in bemusement.

'How can I tell?' was the troll's response. 'No doubt in time you will find out, but let's concentrate on the task at hand which is escaping any encounters with you know who! But first we must rest. It's about five hours till sunrise so I'll take the first watch,' said the generous troll, 'and I will wake you in four hours and then you can let me sleep for an hour before dawn. You see, I do not need as much sleep as humans do'.

The troll looked intently at the boy as he slept. It was true that he had encouraged Garth to try to discover what the stream had gifted him, but all the time the wily old fellow had known what the gift was. He had seen it in essence in the boy's eyes when they had met for the first time on the bridge. He knew that the water of The Crystal Stream had greatly increased it and he surmised that the gift of courageous dedication to duty would be further crafted and strengthened over time as Garth consciously — or unconsciously — nurtured it.

Refreshed by sleep and a quick breakfast of bread, cheese and water, the two friends set out down the mountain with the sketchy plan of heading for a castle lower down where the king sometimes spent time when he was not living in his palace on the Great Plain. They did not, at this stage, have any other plan. Garth hoped that his sister might be living in the castle and that somehow they could make contact and win her over to the forces of good.

As they set out they reminded themselves that they had to be careful and watch out for the herder who by now would know of Garth's escape and would be trying to re-capture him. The two friends also realised that other forces — the king's interrogator and soldiers — would be searching for them.

The day was cold but clear. There was a weak late autumn sun that was nevertheless strong enough to turn the snow of the previous day into slush, which made their progress down the mountain difficult. It was while they were descending a particularly difficult stretch of shallow rocky outcrop that they heard the clank of armour below them on the mountain. The surrounding rocks were too small to hide behind and there was nowhere to take cover, so the two friends were forced to retreat back up the mountain as fast as the slushy snowy landscape would allow.

They trusted to luck that the party of soldiers had not yet seen them but in spite of their every effort, Garth and the troll were unable to put any meaningful distance between themselves and the approaching patrol. After about two hours, they despondently realised that they had climbed higher than their point of setting out earlier in the morning.

This thought further sapped their energy and they were forced to lie on the ground and rest for a few minutes. As they rose to their feet to set off again Garth let out a stifled cry. The troll looked in the direction of Garth's gaze to see nestled at the base of three mountain peaks a rambling set of buildings that were almost lost in the mountain face. The two friends looked at each other and there was an immediate silent agreement as they hastily set off in the direction of the monastery, for they hoped that they might find sanctuary inside.

The hope of finding a refuge renewed their energy as they ran across open ground to a narrow stream's edge which Garth rightly surmised was the waters of the Crystal Stream. There was the beginning of an icy crust forming on the surface of the water but the two did not hesitate and plunged into the icy stream. Garth was wet to his waist when he got out on the other side but the poor troll, who was shorter than Garth, fared far worse for he was soaking wet up to his furry neck! In one thing the troll had an advantage, however, for as he violently shook his whole body, most of the water came off his fur and landed on Garth. Even in spite of their dangerous situation, the two friends laughed as they hurried towards the monastery gates.

'How will we get the monks to open the gates and let us in?' panted the troll to Garth. To their amazement, however, the huge ancient wooden gates slowly opened. Although this was a welcoming sight, something made the friends hesitate before stepping through the entrance, but lacking any other alternative they entered the large cobblestone courtyard.

The *Arch Enemy*

*S*ilence greeted them. They stood quietly, looking for habit-dressed monks, or for any sign of life at all. They were so occupied with this task that they did not notice the gates closing behind them until they were startled by a loud clunk as the gates drew together.

Looking away from the closed gates, the two at last nodded to each other and started to walk slowly across the ancient paved courtyard towards what looked like the main hall of the monastery. Beaten metal doors barred entrance into the hall but just as suddenly as the outer gates of the monastery had mysteriously opened to let them in, so the doors of the hall slowly opened to reveal an extraordinary, unexpected and amazing sight.

Garth and the troll quickly turned to escape, but without them realising it archers had come behind them, and with their bows fully drawn, barred their way. One archer lowered his bow, stepped forward and propelled them into the hall.

The hall from which they had sought to flee was overwhelming. There were flaming torches bracketed along the length of the walls. Heavy drapes and tapestries with the emblem of the king hung from the roof. Courtiers in rich robes formed a passageway that funnelled down to where the king was seated on a raised dais. Everyone in the hall — the king, courtiers and soldiers — silently stared at the newcomers. The silence added to Garth and the troll's sense of impending doom and they were all but overwhelmed with dread of what was going to happen next.

In spite of his fear, Garth tried to take in the appearance of the dark figure sitting on the throne above his courtiers. The boy noted the staring eyes that were fixed upon them and he took in the cruelty that was only too evident on the monarch's face.

The soldier who had pushed them at the door of the hall, at a nod from the monarch propelled them forward again down the aisle, past the staring faces of the courtiers to a short distance from the base of the throne. Then Garth and the troll were roughly forced into a kneeling position under the frightening gaze of the dark figure on the throne. Garth, overcome with fear, nevertheless remembered that the awesome person sitting on the throne above them was his enemy — the murderer of his parents and many other innocent people — and that it was his quest to overcome him!

The silence was at last broken by the cold and deep voice of the monarch.

'We have been awaiting your arrival — since we learnt of your escape this morning.' Then, focusing entirely on Garth he continued. 'In truth we could say that ever since you were born I have searched the length and breadth of Balkonia to find you! Why do you look so amazed? Ah! You expected to see monks but instead you find your king and his court.'

The thought quickly sprang into Garth's mind and he overcame his fear to say, 'Yes! Where are the monks? What has been done with them?'

'It is not you who ask questions here,' replied the king with menace, 'but me!' He continued, 'Well,' (and here sarcasm in his voice was only too evident), 'life is full of unexpected surprises, eh? Here you are... I search no longer. But I will answer your question this once: the monks are long gone and will not be returning.' Here, there was a perceptible snigger from all who stood in the hall. 'And from time to time we find it necessary to visit this forsaken and desolate place.' The king looked around with evident distain. He paused for a moment or two and then a twisted smile spread over his thin and pinched face as he went on. 'But it is opportune that I am in residence at this time for we must welcome you appropriately.' With this, the king nodded to a group of soldiers standing below and to the left of his throne and gave them the order:

'Tie them up! Take them to the dungeon!'

The soldiers came forward and roughly pulled the hands of the two friends behind their backs and bound them securely.

As they were being dragged away the king said to Garth's receding back, 'How are your grandparents? I will be delighted to meet them again! Where are they hiding?' Silence followed the king's statement but a deep dread took hold of Garth and he mentally steeled himself not to reveal where his grandparents were living no matter what the king should do to him. He remembered the promise that he had made to himself in the stone prison within the cave and he silently repeated it again to himself: *I begged mercy from the herder when I was on the edge of the precipice, but I will never beg for mercy again!*

'You will not tell me, eh'? said the dark figure sitting on the throne. 'Never mind,' he said in a menacing tone, pausing for effect before continuing. 'I believe that you had an appointment with my interrogator — an appointment that you have so rudely avoided.' After a moment or two the king said, 'But it has only been postponed. It will happen tomorrow, and I will attend your interrogation myself with a great deal of pleasure!'

The king rose from his throne and descended to the floor below. The courtiers knelt as the monarch passed them and soldiers came to attention. Arriving at the entrance door of the hall, the king half turned and barked an order. 'No food for the prisoners — and only enough water to keep them alive!' The courtiers, now standing erect, had been silent as the two prisoners were dragged past them. Garth had seen expressions of indifference on their faces and he imagined that they were accustomed to unjust and cruel scenes, but here and there he also saw some faces that registered sympathy for their plight.

Garth rightly surmised that they were being taken down to a dungeon where they would eventually meet the interrogator with his or her tools of interrogation! They must have been dragged down several levels before they were pushed through a set of iron doors and then thrown into a musty and dark cell. It took the two friends a few minutes before they were able to work themselves into a sitting position and adapt to the darkness. Then Garth turned towards the troll and said:

'I am so sorry that I got you into this dreadful situation. It looks like there is only torture and death ahead for us.'

'You humans are so easily downhearted and beaten,' said the troll. 'First, let's concentrate on working these ropes off.' With that the troll edged over to the rough wall and started to rub his ropes against it. Garth, after a second or two, followed his example. They spoke as they worked at their task.

'What do you think has become of the monks who lived here in this monastery?' asked Garth of his friend. 'And I believe the cells where we are now imprisoned were not always dungeons but were once wine cellars, for I can see no reason for monks to have had such places as these. Also, what is the connection between the king and this monastery? It is a mystery.'

'Not as much of a mystery as you might think,' said the troll. 'It would seem, according to a story that I have heard from a cousin of mine, that our present dark monarch was as a youth an interesting mix of values. He was spoilt by his parents and very fond of luxury and power. Yet at one stage in his life he played with ideas of embracing another lifestyle. It was after the death of an uncle who he was very fond of that his thoughts turned to an appreciation of spiritual values. He entered this very monastery as a novice monk. But his previous indolent lifestyle was too ingrained in his system. He would not settle for simple food and he would not do as he was asked; rather demanding that other monks serve his every whim. He hungered for power over others and resorted to bullying them. And then he began to notice the ancient treasures that the monastery had acquired over the centuries. And that was that! The more he thought about them the more he wanted them for himself alone!

'As a monk he was a failure and eventually he was asked to leave the monastery. He was bitter and angry. He left, but returned twice — once with soldiers to kidnap your sister and a second time to expel the monks who had deemed him a failure. From there he has continued along this path of evilness. Through cruelty and ruthlessness he has taken over Balkonia and made himself king. Good people like your family have been destroyed, and many like your grandparents have been forced into hiding.' Here the troll ceased talking. They both stopped working at their ropes and sat in silence for several minutes.

'So, you knew all of this when I first spoke to you on the bridge?' asked Garth. The troll just nodded his head in assent.

It took them an hour to work through the ropes and just as they finished, they heard approaching footsteps. The troll, with athletic grace, jumped up and grabbed a low wooden beam. With effortless motion he wedged himself between the beam that he had grabbed and another running parallel to it. Next, a key was inserted into the lock and a jailer was heard to mutter as he entered:

'Why the order to give them water? They will be dead soon enough.'

Another appointment broken with an interrogator!

There was a look of amazement on the fat jailer's face as the troll landed on his back and grabbed the jug of water he was carrying. With as much force as he could muster (the little fellow was exceptionally strong) he hit the jailer over the head with the jug. With a groan, the man dropped to the floor, unconscious.

'Hey!' said the troll smiling from ear to ear and doing a little dance of joy, 'I haven't lost any of my skills while I have been guarding that silly bridge! Boy, did you see how easily I swung up to the roof with such skill and strength? And what about my whack to his noggin? This fat jailer should be out of this world for a little while, and when he does wake up I'll bet he has a very bad headache!'

'Quick, let's get going, Mr show-off! You can go on about it later when we are a long way from this place!'

Garth and the troll hurried from the cell. Once outside, the troll turned the key in the lock so that the jailer could not get out when he recovered consciousness and alert others of their escape. After a brief consultation, the friends chose not to go back the way they had been dragged but rather take their chances by running down the dungeon corridor away from the direction of the monastery hall. The practical troll had picked up the flaming torch that the jailer had dropped and then they set off at a run.

Before they had gone any great distance they heard an approaching platoon of guards. The friends frantically searched for somewhere to hide and at last found a hollow in the wall where they flattened themselves as much as they could, but not before the troll hid the flaming torch behind another bracketed one on the wall. The little fellow shut his luminous eyes so as not to give their presence away, but still they were panic-stricken, fearing that their efforts to find cover had been heard by the approaching soldiers. Right enough, one of the soldiers told his captain:

'I'm certain I heard scuffling noises ahead of us, sir, and it would have been just about here.'

Sick with anticipation, the friends held their breath as the soldiers lingered in the area to search for the source of the noise. The men shone their flaming torches up and down the corridor and the two thought that they would surely be discovered. Garth had an unbearable desire to cough and his eyes watered from the effort to hold it in. Eventually the officer in charge gave the order for the patrol to move off and the two were free at last to breathe easily.

Emerging from their cover, the troll reclaimed the torch and they set out running again, remembering to be as quiet as possible. After about a hundred metres or so, the tunnel became narrower, and to their dismay, eventually ended at a blank stone-face.

'What on earth do we do now?' demanded Garth.

'I know that your eyes are not as good as mine but for goodness sake, use what sight you have got!' exclaimed the troll. 'Look closely at the even cracks around the wall. Just like the stone-face back in the cave, it's a disguised door!'

Garth moved closer and peered at the stone slab which barred their way. It took some time for the boy to see the thin, even markings which indicated a door.

'You're right!' he said. 'Let's get to work and find out how we can open it. Maybe it also operates in the same way as the door in the Crystal Stream Cave.'

The two of them searched by the light of the torch till Garth discovered a lever to the right of the crack and then pulled it. The stone-face started to slide laboriously open and the friends, after a moment's hesitation, squeezed through the opening.

'Well at last, you are of some use!' said the troll 'but don't forget to close it again, boy!' Garth quickly found the lever on the other side of the door and did just that.

*P*risoners *A*gain!

*T*he room on the other side of the stone door was extremely cavernous and their torch was not able to light it sufficiently, so it took a second or two for them to be aware of the shadows. The shadows, they realised, were thrown up on the walls by the light of their own torch, and they were moving!

Garth and the troll stood stock still, their senses alert and ready for anything. The shadows were no longer visible and Garth reckoned that whoever they belonged to had disappeared into crevices in the walls. Yet muffled whispers could be heard… Who or what was in the room with them? Garth grabbed the lighted torch off the troll and held it up high, but the light that it gave did not extend far enough — certainly not into the crevices from where the whispers came.

Suddenly, there was a loud order from the shadowed depths.

'Get them, now!' From out of the darkness a group of figures ran directly at them. There was noise and confusion and the two found themselves knocked to the ground with thrusting, punching bodies on top of them.

They cried out in protest but to no avail! They were being tied up again, and in spite of the danger and helplessness of their situation, Garth was overwhelmed with anger and he screamed out in frustration. 'No, not again! How many times must I be tied up?'

They struggled furiously, and then the apparent leader of the group (who was a tall and very fit woman) said:

'Why are we bothering? If they resist further let's kill them here and now!'

When they heard this order, Garth and the troll stopped struggling immediately! Still, Garth was angry and frustrated but he knew that the leader was serious about the order to kill them so he kept his fury contained. 'First the cattle herder took me prisoner, then the soldiers of the king and now you — whoever you are,' he said in a controlled voice.

At this, the leader of the armed patrol, who was referred to as Juget, stopped giving instructions and peered at Garth by the light of a torch. 'What do you mean? Are you saying that you are not in the service of the king?'

'Of course I am not. I am his sworn enemy! Who are you?' said Garth, and he started to struggle against the ropes once more.

There was silence for some time as the group regarded the struggling boy and his companion. Eventually, Garth stopped his useless wrestling of the ropes, settled into silence and looked at his captors.

'Well, well,' said their leader at last as she held a torch closer to the two in order to examine them. She sucked in her breath, and after a pause, continued. 'What we have here is hardly elite soldiers of the king — just a boy and a troll, certainly not worth all that frantic effort,' she chuckled. The members of the patrol joined in with her laughter, but then they became more serious again as they tried to reason how the boy and his companion had accessed the tunnel. One of the group, a tall strong muscular and rugged man said:

'I'm not so sure of their innocence. They need to be questioned at length!' There were mutters of agreement from the rest, and after a brief discussion they untied the legs of their captives and the group set out prodding and pushing their prisoners along through a series of underground passageways. There was one brief opportunity for a short rest while they waited for three of their group to pull a large stone away from an entrance and then they were all out in the chill night air.

Garth breathed the fresh air deep down into his lungs and he looked up at the star-filled sky. Here at least were his friends — the subject of his contemplation over many clear nights — and he took some comfort from them. The sight of the stars was denied him when the order to blindfold them was given by the group leader. Though the blindfold took away his sight of the stars, it gave Garth some hope about their future. He whispered to his friend, 'They do not want us to see where we are going so there is a chance that they no longer intend to kill us.'

'Silence!' said Juget in a firm harsh tone. 'Under no circumstances must you speak. Soldiers are everywhere tonight. We will despatch you into the next world without hesitation if you give our presence away to our enemies. Do you understand?' The two nodded their heads to show that they would co-operate.

By Garth's reckoning it took about six hours to reach their destination and the concentration needed to stop from falling exhausted the blindfolded pair. At last the cloth ties were removed and they found themselves in the centre of a large courtyard which was surrounded by what appeared to be old and ramshackle buildings.

Among Friends at Last

Gone were the stars of the night before and the sun was some distance across the sky when the two prisoners were taken into one of the buildings, which was in effect more like a meeting hall. The hall had a roof and four walls but there were large areas where there was evidence of repair with apparently whatever make-do materials had been available. On the whole, the building appeared to be weatherproof and in reasonable shape. In one corner was a very large stack of sleeping mats on top of each other, similar to those used by the farming families down on the plain. There was a robust fire burning in a large fireplace at one end of the hall and straddling the fire was an iron triangle on which hung a very large caldron of simmering soup. Next to the fire were rough-hewn tables on which were stacked piles of earthenware bowls, plates and spoons.

It had been some considerable time since the friends had eaten and the smell coming from the pot was delicious. Garth was ravenous but out of a sense of pride averted his gaze from the pot so that the growing number of their captors would not know just how hungry he was. The troll, however, stared at it longingly.

The boy focused on a group of people at the end of the hall. The majority of the group were men, some of whom were wearing the habits of monks. Some women were sprinkled through the group, and the overall impression was one of weather-beaten fitness. The woman called Juget, was addressing the group, and occasionally glances were made by all in their direction.

Garth wondered if there was some connection between the monks who were present in the hall and the ones who had been expelled from the Monastery of The Three Peaks. At any rate, the lad strained hard to hear what was being said but the conversation was just out of earshot. At last the group of about ninety to hundred people came towards them and the two friends found themselves at the centre of a very large, intimidating circle.

'Well, you apparently maintain that you are not in the king's service, but we want to know how you got in the tunnels and why you were there.' These remarks came from a tall and rugged figure who bore many scars on his brawny arms (and one particularly nasty scar down the left-hand side of his weather-creased face). Thoughts rushed through Garth's mind. *Who were these people? Were they really enemies of the king? And for that matter, where should his own story start? How much should he tell them?*

As Garth deliberated, an elderly figure wearing the habit of a monk stepped forward and addressed the group.

'Come, come, sisters and brothers. Before we were warriors we were simple farmers and many of us were spiritual people who were dedicated to meditation and good works. It was one of our beliefs, as farmers and monks, that travellers should always be shown hospitality. We should untie these young folk and offer them some nourishment, for they look famished and exhausted!'

Garth thought that the thick soup was the best food he had ever tasted in his whole life and in spite of his original intention not to show how hungry he was, the boy held out his wooden bowl for a second helping. The troll, however, consumed three bowls without drawing breath and seemed oblivious to the amused stares of their captors.

Somehow the courtesy of the old monk and the humanness of watching the boy and the troll satisfy their basic hunger lightened the atmosphere in the hall and the new elements of goodwill, which Garth perceived, gave him the courage to ask the brawny warrior: 'Who are you, anyway? And by what right do you take us as prisoners?'

'You are hardly in a position to question us,' said the scar-faced leader. He hesitated for a moment or two as he regarded the helplessness yet pluckiness of the two before him. Then with a shrug of his wide shoulders he said, 'What have we to lose? You are our prisoners and perhaps you too may prove to be like us: enemies of the king.' He began the story of the mixed group surrounding the boy and the troll.

'Some of us here are monks who survived the taking of the Monastery of The Three Peaks; others of us are rebels from down on the plains. We have all joined together as guerrilla fighters. Well, that is not entirely accurate — some monks will not take up arms to fight the king's forces as they hold that their spiritual beliefs will not permit them to do so — but they assist the cause in other ways. Other monks are prepared to compromise their individual beliefs by taking up arms for the greater good of eventually bringing our land back to a state of peace and wellbeing.'

There was at this point some commotion at the entrance to the hall as someone called out: 'Taymore! Taymore! A word, if you please.' A man wearing a faded monk's habit made his way through the group and stepped forward directly in front of the scarred warrior who Garth now knew was called Taymore.

The monk whispered something in Taymore's ear and they earnestly looked at the two prisoners before them. After a short pause Taymore continued with his story.

'We took refuge in the secret maze of tunnels that spreads out and under the Monastery of the Three Peaks. Sadly a section of these tunnels has been discovered by the enemy and they use them as a prison. They think that they have discovered the full extent of the tunnel network and do not realise that it is far more extensive.'

Here his story was interrupted by the excited troll who could not contain himself any longer and broke out into a sort of excited jumping dance while chanting: 'We are on the same side! We are on the same side! The dark master and his forces are our enemies, too!'

'I believe you, I believe you,' said Taymore, picking up the repeating pattern of speech from the excited troll and at the same time patting the troll on his furry head. 'Brother Francis here tells me that you are the two that helped the prisoners locked up by the king in the cave system of The Crystal Stream. Our beloved Brother Thomas — the man who was chained to the wall and was very near to death and is even now in our makeshift infirmary — has told his carers, Brother Oliver and Brother Francis (and here he nodded at the monk who had recently interrupted him) the story of how you slowed your own escape in order to release him and others from their cells.'

It was not too long after Taymore's proclamation of their innocence that the two friends found themselves in the same infirmary receiving treatment for their rope burns, many cuts and bruises. Just as importantly, the kind care of the infirmary monks acted as balm for their tired and exhausted spirits.

Comradeship, Training, Study, Vigilance!

The inhabitants of the old monastery were good people dedicated to the return of justice to their land. Living together in the makeshift buildings which had once been a smaller isolated branch of the main Monastery of The Three Peaks, however, was not easy. The members of the group were concerned to be courteous and considerate of their fellows yet conditions were cramped and uncomfortable. It became particularly difficult as autumn passed into winter. Winter, when it came, came quickly.

Yesterday it was still mild enough to venture outside with just one warm cloak over his woollen tunic, but the next day saw a full-blown blizzard, which introduced the harshness of a mountain winter. Garth, who had lived his life on the plains where he had experienced occasional severe winter snowfalls and a frozen river, came to appreciate that here in the mountains there was almost a daily snowfall which added to the depth of the snow lying on the ground from the days before.

The members of the rebel group had made good preparations for the onset of winter. There were outer ramshackle store houses full of provisions which had been given to them by loyal but struggling farmers working down on the Great Plains. There was one storehouse full of vegetables and dried fruits. Another contained grain, ready to be ground into flour for bread, and a remaining storehouse had a variety of salted meats which hung from the ancient rafters.

The large hall, into which they had been brought on that first day, served as a meeting hall, an eating area and sleeping quarters. Garth was glad of the large open fire that blazed away both morning and night and served not only as a source of warmth but as an additional cooking fire. Apart from this hall, the attached kitchen, the blacksmith's shop and the infirmary, the rest of the old dilapidated buildings including the bathhouse and toilet area, were without any form of regular heating.

Garth wondered how such a large group of people avoided being detected by the king's forces, and was told that they were situated well to the west and hours away from the main route up the mountains. They were also told that the rebels had posted lookouts so as to make good their escape to the tunnels under the Monastery of The Three Peaks should soldier patrols ever venture into the region.

'To this point, it has never happened,' said Taymore, 'and we are optimistic that it never will. Still,' he continued, 'we are forever vigilant. Besides, the people down in the foothills of the mountains are loyal to our cause and they would warn us should there be unusual soldier movement outside the main routes of travel.'

Before retiring to the infirmary on that first day, Garth had explained to the rebel army his history and of his membership of the Adagio family. He told the group about his determination to find his sister and his hope of destroying the king.

'Well,' said Taymore, 'you have before you a most difficult quest and we will help you in as many ways as we can, for your intentions run parallel to many of our own.' Here, the warrior paused and then he went on. 'We too seek to do the impossible… What else can we do but try?'

After discussion all agreed that both Garth and the troll should join their group and live and train with them. Each and every morning, no matter how severe the winter weather, Garth, the troll, the rebels and those monks who were prepared to fight, would gather outside in the open to work on their swordsmanship and general fighting skills.

After training with different weapons, Garth's weapon of choice became a short flat sword with edges that had been worked to deathly sharpness in the makeshift blacksmith shop. The blacksmith shop was staffed by leather-aproned monks who worked the great ox-skin bellows to fan the flames of the furnace. Other monks beat out the red hot metal on cast iron anvils.

In practise the boy, like the other warriors, used wooden weapons so as not to blunt in any way the sharpness of his war sword. There was of course also the consideration that no one wanted to hurt a fellow rebel but still, in spite of wooden weapons, injuries did occur from time to time.

Taymore and a young man called Jason were particularly involved in the development of Garth's fighting skills. At first the boy, although fit and strong, was vulnerable to so many sword manoeuvres, but he was intelligent and he worked tirelessly, and even Taymore had to agree that he was making significant progress.

The going was not easy, however, and often Garth's limbs would be screaming for him to stop but he would carry on without giving in to the need for rest. Of course, as time went on it became easier for him to stay the distance and this was helped by a spurt of growing that came after the first months of his joining the rebels.

'Do you expect to meet the king's army in battle one day?' he asked Taymore after they had completed a particularly hard training session.

'No,' the warrior had replied. 'We could never hope to match that big an army in open combat. We can only hope to gain ground if we fight with the protection of the forest and our knowledge of the mountains. Who knows, one day we might be lucky and catch the king with only the protection of a single patrol. So we must be forever ready to take advantage of any opportunity and prepare for that moment by gaining maximum fitness and fighting skills. Our major hope lies in the fact that the people despise the king. While they suffer under his cruelty (to this point they fear his reprisals too much to rise up against him), they admire our resistance, and who knows, events may bring about their actively joining us and then by sheer force of numbers we would eventually beat him.'

Sometimes, late in the evenings, after the youngest of the children had retired for sleep and the basic night meal of vegetable and meat soup along with thick crusty bread was just a pleasant memory, Garth and other young people would sit with the monk who had saved him and the troll from questioning. The monk's name was Francis and he was one who had chosen to support the rebels by assisting them without actually taking up arms.

Francis would teach Garth and the other young people as much as he could from the areas that he had studied over the years. They delved into the books which had been saved from the king's destruction of the monastery library, and Garth came to appreciate that some holy men had perished in their efforts to save the very books that were laid out before them. He was overwhelmed with respect for these monks who had valued learning and knowledge more than their own lives. He remembered also his beloved grandparents — his first teachers — and he recognised many similarities between them and the monks. Garth, who had previously only known the companionship of his grandparents, enjoyed the friendship and camaraderie of the monks, the troll, Jason, Taymore and his band of rebels. Here, among his new companions, he discovered friendship and also reserves of energy in himself that he had not known were there.

The nine women who had chosen to join the rebels had brought their children with them. They knew that the king's men would probably have found them had they been placed with friends or relatives down on the plain. The ages of these children ranged from four to fourteen years and Garth formed a particular friendship with the eldest of the children — a girl named Naomi.

Naomi was tall for her fourteen years. She was the only child of Juget, and like her mother, she had shiny ebony hair, but in many ways she excelled her mother's good looks. Her eyes were deep blue and displayed a softness and gentleness almost out of place with the harsh environment of the dilapidated monastery.

'I am regarded as being a child,' said Naomi one evening after she and the other young people had finished their lessons with Brother Francis, 'but really I am not all that much younger than you.' Many times during those months Garth and Naomi walked together and spoke of normal everyday things — nothing of fighting or quests — and Garth thought that the girl was full of grace and that her company was somehow wonderful.

At times Garth was surprised at how he had changed, for not only had his body become harder and stronger but he had a determined attitude and singularity of purpose that defied the idea of failure, no matter how impossible victory might seem. During the day Garth's optimism was supported by the long training program and the growing friendships he was developing with members of the group, particularly Naomi and the troll.

Naomi was a gifted storyteller and he loved nothing better than to sit close to her by the fire and listen to her stories. Like so many good storytellers before her, she would ask her listeners for an opening line for her tale and from the opening line her wonderful imagination would weave a story. Sometimes he allowed himself to imagine peaceful times — sitting by other homely fires — and always Naomi was there with him, laughing and spinning her wonderful tales.

One still winter's day when he and the troll had paused in their task of cutting wood for the great fire in the hall, Garth had confided in his friend.

'I dream sometimes that when I am older I will have my own comforting fire. I always imagine that Naomi is somehow sitting there with me and we are laughing about the day's events or that she is telling a story.'

'Oh dear!' replied the troll. 'You *are* growing up, aren't you? I hope that there will always be a seat at that fireplace for an ugly old troll!' Garth, laughing, laid his axe on the ground, and putting an arm around his friend's shoulder, said:

'Always!'

He was further buoyed up and distracted by the games that he played with the children before the evening meal. Naomi would watch as he and several of the other young men pretended to be horses, and with the children on their backs would "gallop" up and down the hall getting in the way of those adults trying to set the tables for the evening meal. When the night drew on and all was quiet in the old buildings and the companionship and laughter of friends was silenced, it was often a different matter.

If sleep did not immediately overtake him, Garth would go over the day's events. He would recall the training sessions and the manoeuvres that he had practised. From there, he would go over in his mind the readings and talks that he and Naomi and the other young people had shared with Brother Francis around the fire. Inevitably his thoughts would turn towards his family. A longing to see his grandparents would overtake him and he felt a strong need to ensure himself that they were safe and well. As he lay on his sleeping mat and listened to the deep breathing of his companions, he lost some of the sense of security that he felt during the day and evening, and he was overwhelmed by anxiety at the enormity of the tasks that lay before them.

He wondered too about what his parents had been like, and how his life would have been if he had grown up as part of a larger family — to have a mother, father and yes, a sister. One night when he had been awake and restless for many hours, Garth finally faced up to what he had been previously unwilling to appreciate in all its horror: his mother and father had been murdered and his sister had probably been won over to the side of the murderous king. It was then that a feeling descended on Garth that he could not explain. He hoped with all his might that what he felt in the depth of his being was not cold hatred. It was from this point onwards, however, that Garth's training companions noted that his fighting skills became even more courageous and his dedication even more intense.

Section Two

Rosamund's Story
The Crafting of the King's Examiner

Missing from the Campfire

Rosamund remembered little of her early childhood; there were just some vague and isolated memories. One of those memories was of a group of people whom she surmised had been her family, but the images in her mind were disjointed and vague. The feelings associated with these people, however, were comforting and pleasant.

A slightly stronger memory was of a time when she was on a journey — she thought that the journey involved going up a mountain. She was wrapped up in rugs and sitting on a horse… or was it a donkey? The group that she was with took her to a complex of ancient buildings where she was cared for by kindly men wearing worn brown robes. She was not sure of other details. The memories associated with these events were further muddled by images of flashing weapons and sudden coldness as the security of soft kind voices, and warmness were ripped away from her, and a journey began again — this time down the mountain.

The girl's only remaining link with her early childhood was a pendant that she always wore around her neck under her clothes. She did not know but it was the mirror image of the pendant Garth had found in the box in his grandparent's mud and willow reed cabin.

She did not remember the details of her capture by the king and his forces — only the sense of coldness and the tearing away of warmth — but she had clung to the pendant when a soldier had tried to take it from her.

'Let the child keep it,' said an official. 'What harm can it do? And it seems to give her some comfort.' Rosamund had retained the pendant, and without knowing why, she valued it more than any other of her possessions.

From about the age of five Rosamund's childhood memories developed increasing clarity. For eight months of the year, Rosamund lived in a castle in the foothills of the great mountain range which dominated the plains. During these eight months she was relatively free to do pretty well as she pleased. The remaining four months of the year she lived in the main palace of the king which was situated further south on the central plains.

When she lived in the king's palace, her life was marked by rigorous schedule. Every day she would rise at the same time, and after breakfast, Rosamund worked with a series of tutors. The main tutor and the one with whom she spent the majority of her time taught her the history of their country. These unruly people were referred to as "the rebels." The girl was taught to see the ruling families of the past as enemies of the people whose ambition of returning to power, if successful, would bring nothing but poverty and trouble to the land.

When she lived in the castle in the foothills of the mountain range which ran across the northern regions of Balkonia, things were very different. The building with its surrounding moat was regarded by all as belonging to her, but in spite of her overall control there was still a representative of the king living there and forever watching what was happening. Rosamund, in spite of this man's presence, was free to go riding outside of the walls but her rides were restricted to a circumference of about fifteen kilometres into the countryside. Yet even here, she was not permitted to enter any of the three hamlets that were within the permitted radius.

Rosamund had a beautiful chestnut mare of about sixteen hands and she loved this horse dearly. Most days she would ride out for hours at a time into the surrounding hills and valleys. When the girl returned from her daily ride she would insist on unsaddling and grooming the animal herself till its coat shone with a golden healthy gleam. She would then prepare the mare's feed, and all the while she would speak to it in a soft and gentle voice.

During the eight months when she lived in her castle at the foot of the mountain range she regularly went hunting in a nearby forest. On these hunting expeditions the girl would go on foot, taking along her two beautiful deer hounds who were devoted to her. The old hunting master at the castle was the only person to accompany Rosamund on these hunting trips. At night they would camp with the dogs under the stars; their only comfort a low campfire and a blanket.

The old man had encouraged Rosamund to spend hours practising with her long bow, and as a result, the girl became a very accurate shot. The hunting master emphasised that a wounded animal must always be pursued and put out of its misery — never left to suffer from its wounds.

'If you are successful,' he had told her at the outset of their hunting expeditions, 'and hunt down and kill your prey, you must always skin and prepare it for cooking yourself.' The girl, unused to any physical labour except the grooming of her horse, asked:

'Why must I? Such work is for servants.'

'Well, it is respectful of the life you have taken and it is a form of gratitude for the food that you eat,' he replied. The girl, on some level, appreciated the wisdom of this instruction and so was instructed in the art of skinning her kill and preparing it for cooking.

The old man was silent most of the time during these hunting expeditions except to instruct Rosamund in the art of stalking prey, and the girl found this silence good. One night they were sitting around a crackling fire after a satisfying day's hunt. The air was fresh and still and the sky was ablaze with stars. Rosamund thought there was a quality of deep purple to the night that she had never really appreciated before, and she also understood for the first time that the darkness of the night was not something to fear, but was her friend.

The old hunter wore a thick blanket around his shoulders, and gathering the blanket tighter, he stirred the fire and then turned and looked long and hard at the girl. Rosamund was sitting contentedly on a log and one of the hounds had his head in her lap. She was stroking his strong shaggy neck.

'The night is perfect, isn't it?' said the girl, responding to the hunter's look.

'No,' was the reply. The girl was puzzled.

'Why? What is lacking?' The man was silent for some time and then said:

'I wish things were different. I wish your father was alive and here with us… and your brother… he should be here, too. Then the night would be perfect.'

Rosamund looked at the old hunter in amazement but when she sought to question him further he mumbled, 'I have said too much already,' and he left the campfire and moved off into the forest, not returning till dawn the next morning. Without speaking about the matter further, they returned to the castle.

Rosamund, however, thought about the hunter's words constantly but she bided her time until an opportunity presented itself on the next hunting expedition.

'On our last hunting trip, what did you mean when you said that my father and brother were missing?' she asked the huntsman.

'If you ever refer again to what I said that evening I will no longer go with you on hunting trips and I will leave the castle for ever,' was his serious and yet pleading reply. Rosamund, who valued his presence and skills very much, knew that she must respect his wishes and not talk to him, or anyone else, about the matter. She did, however, make one exception and spoke to an old and trusted servant called Petra who had been with her almost as far as her memory extended.

Living in The King's Palace on the Great Plain

It was late one evening and Petra, under Rosamund's instructions, was packing some personal items that she intended to take on their yearly journey to the king's palace on the Great Plain.

'I do not look forward to going down on the plain for there are so many things that I love about this place,' said the girl looking out of the window into the deep mellow night. 'More than anything else though, I will miss my hunting trips into the forest with my dogs and the old huntsman, Leopold.' She paused before continuing. 'You know, Petra, several hunting trips back he said an extraordinary thing to me. We were sitting by the fire and it was an evening just like tonight — perfect! The stars were out and the evening air was chilly but pleasant.

'I thought that Leopold felt the evening was perfect too, but when I mentioned this to him he said something about it lacking the presence of my father and brother.' Here the girl paused and then after a few moments took up the subject again.

'I have since asked him to explain his comments but his only response was to say that I must never speak again of the matter. What do you make of what he said, Petra?'

Petra had not looked up during the girl's confidence but she had paused in her packing. Then she had resumed her task and at last looked up and said:

'I have no idea what he meant. He is getting past it, I think, and inclined to ramble on about a whole lot of nothings.

'Well, I have finished packing what you asked me to include. Will there be anything else tonight, your grace?'

'No, there is nothing else. Thank you, and goodnight.'

There was still a little time to go before leaving for the plains and Rosamund, after making all her preparations for departure, expressed her intention to go on an overnight hunting excursion into the forest, southwest of the castle.

'Sadly, you will not be able to go with your regular huntsman,' said Petra, 'because a few evenings ago he had an unfortunate accident and fell on his own spear when he was out hunting.'

Rosamund, who had been reading, looked up, amazed at the idea that the capable huntsman could have made such an error as to fall on his own spear.

'I told you he was past it, didn't I? said Petra. 'Well, we will see who else we can find to accompany you, shall we?' The woman left the room. The girl was inclined to give into a feeling of sadness over Leopold but she was self-centred and resisted this inclination, and set about distracting herself.

Rosamund did not look forward to the four months in the king's palace. She greatly missed the freedom of long rides on her beautiful chestnut mare. Gone too was the freedom of days and nights in the forest. Instead she was locked into a strict daily routine which varied little except for the days when she had meetings with the king.

Her daily routine involved lessons with various tutors, particularly a history teacher who spent long periods explaining the evils of the past under the governance of the old families. Rosamund found these lessons repetitive and boring, but she really looked forward to her music lesson. Under this teacher she learnt the lute and an ancient wooden instrument not dissimilar to a flute called a trevent. Sometimes, when their music lesson was over the tutor, whom Rosamund liked the best out of all her instructors, would recite poetry to her. This he did furtively out of the hearing of any servants or palace officials.

The tutor's memory was good and the poems were long and wonderfully lyrical, and she had the vague idea that they referred to her own country and the ruling families of the past. They spoke of brave and noble actions, of honour and virtue tested and rewarded, and Rosamund loved them. She wondered, however, if the poems referred to her own country, how the content in the poems were reconcilable with the history that she was taught. She came to the conclusion that they were just lyrical flights of fancy.

Several hours in the afternoon were devoted to physical fitness and martial arts, particularly swordsmanship. Twice a week her fitness routine involved a long run around the palace grounds. It was near to the end of her third month on the Plain when Rosamund experienced something that secretly worried and distressed her.

One afternoon when they were jogging along, her fitness instructor caught the eye of a girl who Rosamund surmised he very much admired. As he stopped to talk to her, Rosamund stood at a distance so that she would not hear what they were saying. Then the fitness tutor said, 'Your Grace, you go on ahead and I will catch you up.' Rosamund then ran on, picking up her speed, exhilarated at the prospect of running alone without a constant companion.

As the girl ran past the stables near a set of minor gates in the palace walls, she noticed that a side gate had been opened to allow a group of horses to be led through. Several of the horses were plunging and shying, and were difficult to control. There was a great deal of shouting and pulling in order to get them to pass through the open gates. In the confusion of controlling the spirited horses, the gate was not immediately closed. Curiosity about town life that she had not experienced overcame her, and the girl quickly slid through the opening to the world outside.

Rosamund soon noticed the stares that she received from the people she passed. At first she wondered why and then it hit her in a flash: it was the clothes that she was wearing! She was dressed in loose fitting pants, a silk top and soft leather shoes, all of which allowed her to exercise and run in freedom. Although the style of her dress caused some attention, it was their quality that contrasted starkly with that of the ordinary folk surrounding her. They were so obviously poor; their clothes were thin and worn. She noted that the people appeared thin and worn, too.

Rosamund wandered away from the palace in an easterly direction, but her time outside the palace walls was limited — perhaps to an hour at most. A patrol of soldiers located her in a busy market square and she was bundled unceremoniously into an enclosed litter, similar to the one in which she travelled with her two deer hounds and Petra from her castle to the palace each year.

There was an enormous fuss about the incident and Rosamund's fitness instructor was replaced immediately by three unbending and hardened soldiers. When the girl asked the three soldiers what had happened to her old instructor her enquires were met with a stony silence, but there were meaningful glances exchanged among his replacements and Rosamund suspected that he had been badly dealt with.

The girl felt some regret for the removal of her instructor, his only crime being his stopping to flirt with a palace serving girl thereby leaving her unattended for a few minutes. She was also very much puzzled by what she had observed during the time that she was outside the palace grounds. She told herself over and over that her time outside had been brief and that what she saw may not have represented a true picture of life among the ordinary people. The images of poverty, the ragged appearance of people, the absence of good food products on the stalls in the marketplace, and the groups of chained men, women and even children ready to be sold into slavery in the town square, stayed in her thoughts.

These things were at odds with the luxury she enjoyed in her own life. The poverty was also at odds with what her tutors and the king told her about the state of the country outside. The girl, however, had been brought up in a world where all her whims were met and she did not spend too much time on sympathy or care for others. The end result was that although she had been unnerved by the poverty and pain that she had encountered in her time outside the palace walls, in the long term she allowed the unpleasant images to fade away.

On occasions there were meetings with the king himself. Sometimes these meetings were conducted with full ceremony with the king surrounded by all the pomp and splendour of his court. The girl was instructed to kneel before the king on a red cushion at the base of the stair leading to his throne, and offer him a statement of loyalty and subservience. For a week before these meetings, Rosamund was tutored on protocol. Every detail from her entrance into the throne room to her leaving it was gone over in tiresome detail. Even the way she should walk down the long throne room was minutely stipulated.

On other occasions she met with the king privately in a pavilion in the grounds of the palace, and at these meetings the king's manner lacked any tone of officialdom. They even had refreshments together. Rosamund privately thought that at these meetings the king's manner was over-friendly and he seemed very eager to please her. She wondered why. She imagined, at times, that he might even be willing to grant her every wish.

Rosamund considered once or twice asking the king if she could be taken on a visit to the outside world, but in spite of his friendliness there was an underlying sinister streak in the man which prevented her from making this particular request. It was this same awareness of his disguised cruelty that also prevented her from asking him about the poor conditions that she had encountered on her brief visit to the outside world.

The difference between the meetings where the king was surrounded by his courtiers and their private meetings, remained extremely puzzling to the girl. She felt at times that it was important to the king that his courtiers see that she was only a tool and under his power, while at their private meetings she had a sense that it was somehow *she* who had the real power. She thought long and hard about why the king was concerned to please her. While she took for granted the luxury and privilege that surrounded her, she wondered at times who she was and where she had come from.

Her servant, Petra, was closer to Rosamund than any other person. The girl thought of her as more of a friend than a servant, and she often shared her thoughts with her. One night, as Petra was brushing the girl's gleaming, long black hair before plaiting it for sleep, Rosamund confided in her, in much the same way as she had previously spoken about her puzzlement over the statements made by the old huntsman Leopold about the absence of her father and brother. She told the servant about the time she had spent outside the precincts of the palace.

'Did you know that several weeks ago when I was running in the palace grounds, I took the opportunity to slip through some gates and I spent about an hour outside the palace walls?'

'No, I didn't know that,' said Petra with an air of surprise.

'Well, I did — and you know, Petra, what I saw has worried me a little.'

'Why has it worried you, your grace?'

'Well, I expected it to be different somehow. I mean, there was no laughter and… and,' here the girl hesitated before continuing, 'the people looked so poor. As I wandered among the stalls in the marketplace I could see the poverty of the people. Some even looked hungry. And then I noticed an old lady looking at me very carefully.

'She came from behind a stall that was selling what looked like second-hand clothes, and she made her way over to where I was standing. After coming up close to my face and staring at me intently, she asked if I was a member of the Adagio family. I honestly was taken aback and didn't know how to respond! She pleaded with me to save our country. It all happened so quickly,' said the girl. 'Just as she said this to me, I was discovered by soldiers and they bundled me into a litter. She called after me, crying out that she had known and loved my mother. "You and your brother are our only hope of salvation", she screamed just before one of the soldiers hit her with a club and she fell to the ground. I don't know what happened to her after that because the curtains were pulled closed on the litter, but I do know that the soldier certainly hit her with a vicious blow and I doubt that she would have survived it.'

Initially, Petra was transfixed but then said, 'Well, don't mind things like that. You are entirely mistaken. The people are happy and under the best of rulers,' and she gave Rosamund a reassuring squeeze on her shoulders. 'The old lady was undoubtedly a lunatic and you are lucky that the soldiers pulled you away before she could do you harm. She may well have been a thief with a hidden knife. You don't know how it might have ended.'

After a space of a few minutes, during which the nurse brushed the girl's hair in a somewhat agitated manner, Rosamund said, 'Well, where do I come from? Am I a member of the Adagio family? Do I have a brother? It is the second time that I have heard that I have a brother. Do you remember? I told you that the old hunting master, Leopold, mentioned that my father and brother were missing from our forest campfire.'

'What nonsense are you speaking,' the servant said in a somewhat high-pitched tone. 'You should go to bed immediately so as to be fresh for your meeting with the king tomorrow.' Something in the woman's manner made Rosamund look up in surprise and from that point an uncomfortable silence developed between them. Soon after, the girl went to bed.

The meeting was to be early in the morning because the king was setting out on a journey to the mountains later on that day. Rosamund made every effort to go to sleep so as to be fresh for the encounter, but the girl was uneasy and restless, and sleep evaded her till quite late into the night.

A Spy and Not a Friend!

Rosamund rose early for her meeting with the king. She thought that arriving ahead of time would allow her to sit at a short distance from the pavilion and look at the peace and beauty of the lake. She hoped that by so doing she might regain some of the calmness that had disappeared the night before when she had told Petra about her time outside the confines of the palace. She had been surprised, and pleased, at her servant's absence when she got out of bed that morning as it allowed her to concentrate on trying to recover from the agitation of the night before.

There was no wind and the lake was indeed calm and peaceful. There was a wispy mist that rose from its surface. The sun, only a short distance over the horizon, held the promise of a warm and pleasant day. Rosamund sat on a grassy slope a short distance from the picturesque pavilion where the meeting with the king was to take place. After looking at the pavilion and wondering how the meeting would go, she turned away to look at the lake and drink in the peace of the early morning.

It was a doe and her fawn. Disturbed perhaps by something further away in the nearby forest, something sent them thumping out of a stand of trees behind the pavilion and made the girl look in their direction. She was at once astounded to see Petra, emerging from the king's garden pavilion and scurrying away across the parkland towards the main palace buildings. Knowledge came to Rosamund in a flash and she spoke the words out aloud (perhaps because it was too much of a burden to keep the knowledge inside.) 'So… that is how he knows so much about me! I have trusted Petra and now I know that she tells the king everything that I say and do! She is no friend to me, but an informant… a spy!'

All the peace that she had gained in the last half hour was gone and replaced instead by a sickening feeling of unease and anger. Thoughts came rushing in. She remembered the old hunting master's sudden death from a spear wound which he supposedly had inflicted on himself by accidently falling on his weapon. At the time she had been amazed that such an experienced hunter could be so careless as to fall on his own weapon.

'Oh dear,' she said out aloud, 'he told me not to mention what he said around the campfire — about my father and brother being absent from our hunting party… and… and I confided in Petra. I betrayed him! I probably caused his death!'

The girl sat there for a long time, but when the bell signalling the end of the early morning watch sounded, Rosamund rose from the grassy mound and made her way to the king's garden pavilion. The guards at the entrance announced her presence and she was allowed to enter.

'Come in, come in, Rosamund. Have you had breakfast yet? I think not. Come and have breakfast with me,' said the king in a good humour. Rosamund refused everything but a hot drink and this she had in order to settle the uneasy feeling that she had in her stomach. After the king had finished his own breakfast and the remains had been cleared away, he settled back and looked steadily at the girl before saying:

'Well, Rosamund, I have been informed that you have been sitting outside for some time, so we will not pretend, eh? You saw your servant woman leaving and you now know that she is entirely faithful to me — as you also should be — for have I not always been good to you and looked after your every need?' His statement had progressively adopted a hard tone.

'I am disappointed, sir. I have always been loyal to you. There has never been the need for spies,' responded the girl in an equally hard voice.

The king looked at Rosamund for several moments and then said, 'Be that as it may. The time has come for hard talking between us and firm agreement. It is irrelevant as to whether you identified your servant as my informant or not, for I have intended that in this meeting you should learn of my plan for you and that you should set out with me this very afternoon for the carrying out of that plan. You want to know who you are and why you are under my protection. Well, I will tell you the story of how you came to be here and why we must work together for our troubled land of Balkonia.'

What followed was a story that is the most dangerous of all stories: one of half-truths.

Rosamund's Early History "Revealed" to Her

The king told Rosamund that he had been a member of an ancient royal family which had ruled the land for many years, but then there had been a revolution set up years before he was born by a group of families and lead by an old wizard. The revolution had resulted in his own family being deposed and replaced in governorship by a council consisting of two members from each of the main revolutionary families. They ruled badly and were only concerned for the wealth and welfare of their own families. The wizard who led them in their revolution gave one of the governing families special powers. Here, the king paused for effect. 'In every seventh generation, the first born — if a girl — is particularly powerful.'

'Was that family called the Adagio family?' asked Rosamund.

'Well, yes,' said the king. 'Why do you ask?'

'When I ventured outside the palace walls I encountered an old lady in a market square who said that I was of that family… and… she also said that she had known and loved my mother… and… and that I have a brother!'

'I know of the incident and that woman has been dealt with in the way that all troublemakers will be dealt with. However, she did give us some useful information before she died and I will return to this information after I have told you some more of our history.'

Rosamund thought that she detected a cruel expression on the king's face as he said the words that the old lady had 'been dealt with.' She was also puzzled by how the old woman had looked — she somehow had not fitted the image of a troublemaker worthy of being killed. She had appeared more like a troubled person pleading for help for herself and others. The girl fought the distraction to further think about that day in the market square because the king was continuing his story.

'After many generations of rule by these families it was necessary for my father to defeat them in battle and take back the right to be king because you see Rosamund, Balkonia was in a dreadful state. There had been succeeding years of failed harvests but the people were still over taxed and no consideration was ever given to their increasingly poor circumstances. Yet,' continued the king, 'the ruling families themselves lived in obscene luxury!'

At this point, Rosamund was tempted to say that they themselves lived rather well and that the people outside the palace appeared to be still poor! She realised that her observation had been fleeting and that she could indeed be wrong. Besides, she knew that such comments would not be welcomed by the man sitting before her. Against this internal observation was the thought that she should trust the judgement of the king who had allowed her to lead such a comfortable and privileged life.

The king continued. 'I mentioned the old sorcerer, didn't I? Well, he was on the side of the ruling families and he gave some restricted mystical power to all members of the Adagio family to go down with them through the ages... but... but he made the special provision for a significant amount of power to be given to the firstborn of every seventh generation — if a girl.' Here the king paused momentarily in his story to look intently into Rosamund's eyes, and he saw a flicker of illumination as the girl finally understood who she was and why the king controlled her life.

'Yes, you have guessed correctly, Rosamund: you are a firstborn of a seventh generation. And you do have a special power in you that will only emerge when you travel high into the mountains and drink at a certain stream. You are the one good fruit born of a family who cares nothing for the welfare of our people. I, on the other hand, have been completely dedicated to the welfare of our people and in regard to you... well, I have cared and nurtured you almost from your birth and... and... trust me, there are many who would have destroyed you years ago because of your membership in the Adagio family, but I have been your protector.

'As confirmed by the old woman who you encountered in the marketplace in recent times, the rebels have been reorganising. They train somewhere in the mountains and are increasing in number. They sustain their needs by raiding the poor farmers of the plains who live in fear of the rebels regaining power.'

The king then stopped talking, allowing the girl to take on board all that he had told her. Rosamund could not but spare a thought for the old lady who must have suffered before giving up the piece of information that the rebels were re-arming and preparing for rebellion.

But the old lady had seemed genuine. Why had she been on the side of the rebels? she wondered. She wondered also just how much truth was in the words of the monarch and how much he was trying to manipulate her thoughts. Then the king broke the silence.

'It is time now for you to recognise my kindness over the years. It is time for you to join me in my work to rid this land of dissenting rebels. I wanted to wait one or two more years but we have been overtaken by events and I must make my move now.

'I will take you to drink at the waters of The Crystal Stream and then announce to all the people who you are and your commitment to me. You are committed to me, are you not?' said the king in a low voice.

'Indeed, I am grateful to you for all your care and protection over the years.' Rosamund looked away from

the man sitting in front of her for a reflective moment
and then returned her gaze to his. 'What is this special
power, sir, which will be given to me?'

'Well, you will have to wait and see,' said the
monarch in a low voice.

At this point a servant entered the pavilion, and at
a word from the monarch, approached him and
whispered something in his ear. The king nodded his
approval and then turned to the girl. 'As a gesture of our
understanding, Rosamund, you will no longer be
troubled by the presence of the informer, Petra. She has
been removed from your service.'

The girl did not dwell on the fate of her serving
woman for whom she now only felt dislike and
resentment. It did not occur to her that the woman had
only been a tool, much as Rosamund was now allowing
herself to be. It was the beginning of coldness of heart
that would grow over time with her service to the king.
This coldness would further be fed by the enjoyment of
her increased power and the awe and fear in which she
would be held by all who surrounded her.

'Rosamund, it is your destiny to join me in
greatness,' said the king. 'Go back to your rooms and
make arrangements, for we leave this very day! You are
to accompany me to the mountains where you will drink
at the Crystal Stream. You will discover your special
power and we will find a suitable title for you. We will
give you tasks that will demonstrate to all the people
that you are my dedicated and trusted partner!'

As the girl looked at the animated man, she suspected that he already knew what her gift would be. Indeed he did know! The title that he planned to give her was The Examiner for she would gain the task of searching for disloyalty in the hearts and minds of all who surrounded the king.

Section Three

The Sorcerer's Gifts
Courage is Crafted in Adversity

Plans and Strategies

It was at this point that the Rebels started to appreciate that the time for training was over and the time for action had arrived. Information had come to them from their contacts (both in the palace and in the king's court) that the king was determined to make an all-out effort to destroy any resistance to his control. Jason had returned from a visit to the plains with the information that the monarch was putting boasting that he would soon have a "secret weapon" that would legitimise and support his reign. In conjunction with this boast he was organising additional patrols to search out where the rebels lived and trained in the mountains. 'While he does not know where we live and train,' said Jason to Taymore, 'he does appear to have an idea of the region, so he will mount bigger and bigger searches till he finds us. So to my reckoning, Taymore, timing is very important.'

Armed with these developments, Taymore called a meeting of the whole company at the monastery. They gathered an hour or so after the evening meal when all the children had been put to bed. The council of war saw the leaders sitting around a long table in the centre of the hall and the rest of the company standing around within hearing and consulting distance. The fire was burning steadily and this, along with bowls of a strong sweet drink which was Brother Charles's speciality for important occasions, gave them some comfort for whatever lay ahead.

After an initial silence of some minutes, Taymore said, 'Well, my friends, we all know that we do not stand a chance against such overwhelming odds. The king's army outnumbers us three hundred to one at least, and they also have superior equipment. Their archers number perhaps more than five hundred men,' and here he paused before continuing, 'and let us be honest, they are extremely well trained and deadly accurate.

'So, what do we have? We have absolute dedication. I believe that the forces of good are on our side — and that surely is worth a great deal. Our warriors will fight more bravely than the king's soldiers because we believe in what we are fighting for. We have unparalleled knowledge of mountain terrain and we can read mountain conditions and weather. Furthermore, our training has prepared us to melt back into the landscape and escape, should circumstances dictate it to be the appropriate strategy. The onset of melting snow will create difficult soggy fighting conditions and this will also suit our purposes and particular fighting skills, but,' here he paused for effect, 'what we really need is for the people to rise up and join us — that would make all the difference! We would not lose, then!'

What followed was a reflective silence as the company thought over what Taymore had said. Brother Charles and his helpers took the opportunity to go around and refill empty bowls with his special steaming brew.

'The people are afraid of the king, and with good enough reason,' continued Taymore. 'Amongst the general populace he is known as The Dark Master and there is not a family who has not experienced in some way his brutality. Any resistance to his wishes has been put down with ruthless force and not only has the individual been punished, but the person's family has also been subject to retaliation. So as a result, the people will not rise up too easily, and certainly not unless they can be sure of eventual success.'

'What are we to do?' asked Garth, who because of his position as a member of the Adagio family and also because of his tremendous progress in training as a warrior, had been given a seat at the table. The troll who was for ever at Garth's side, sat on the floor near his friend's knee. Taymore thought for a moment and then replied.

'In a way, Garth, we must trust to fate, creating the circumstances which will make the people rise up. We must make a leap of faith, if you like, and hope that our example of self-sacrifice will trigger courage in the people, and that they will put aside fear and give us actual physical support.'

So what followed was a discussion that went on through the night till the pale winter sun came up over the mountain range. All members of the group were free to offer suggestions about possible strategies, and all opinions were treated seriously and with respect. The end result was a campaign that would employ the following range of strategies: when deliberately meeting up with an enemy patrol, they would seek to entice the soldiers to follow them deep into the mountains by appearing to be overwhelmed by the possibility of engagement defeat. Ambushes would be set up for the king's men well in advance of any such action.

Another strategy to be employed was to have two groups of rebels attack — one from the front and another from the rear. The surprise element would assist the rebels to best utilise this pincer attack and would initially throw the enemy into disarray. This plan involved retreating back into the cover of rocks and crevices so as to make good their escape before the enemy could regain order. It was also thought that army patrols camping out at night would make easy targets for guerrilla tactics.

'We hit them suddenly and hard,' said Juget, 'and then disappear into the night.'

There were also plans to make occasional forays down into the enemy heartland itself. This would be completely unexpected and any successful raids would give the rebels a fearless reputation as fighters, assisting them in their efforts to gain the hearts and minds of the people. Of course, such raids would need the help of loyalists faithful to the rebels' cause. These loyalists would need to be capable of hiding the rebels until it was safe for them to retreat back up into the mountains.

They reasoned that any engagement should not be anywhere in the region of their monastery camp. Plans were also made for retreating into the tunnels under the Monastery of the Three Peaks further up the mountain in the event of their camp being discovered. Of particular concern was the safety of the children. It was necessary, they sadly reasoned, that a party should set out a week or two before their campaign began to take the ten children to the safety of the neighbouring country of Scarpland, to people who were sympathetic to their cause.

All of those present agreed that their campaign should begin in the first weeks of spring, which was still several weeks away. Then the whole company (excluding the lookouts) retired for a few hours of sleep before turning to the duties of the day.

Rosamund Drinks the Waters of
The Crystal Stream

The king's caravan set out in the early afternoon. Rosamund's preparations had been hurried but the monarch's had not. Pomp and splendour were evident, and the girl who would have preferred to ride a horse was forced to travel in a sedan chair that was heavily curtained and carried by ceremonial guardsmen.

The journey to the mountains took several days, and each night they were entertained at the estates of aristocrats in the king's service. During the night meal the monarch always told his host that the primary reason for their journey to the high country was for Lady Rosamund to drink the waters of The Crystal Stream. Rosamund noticed that when the monarch — apparently in a casual way — mentioned the purpose of their journey, there were often meaningful glances shared between those sitting at the table. (She reasoned that some of these glances contained elements of anxiety and even fear.)

They are somehow threatened by the gift that I will receive when I drink the waters of The Crystal Stream.

I do not know what I will receive, but perhaps they do.
The girl found it all very puzzling.

In the fullness of time, Rosamund found herself kneeling on the cushion that had been ceremoniously placed at her feet at the water's edge. The monarch, sitting on a portable throne under a gold tasselled canopy, turned and nodded to the captain of his personal guard. The soldier went to the saddlebag on his horse and took from it a gold cup and presented it to the kneeling girl. Rosamund knew that she was expected to dip it into The Crystal Stream and then drink from it.

Her heart was pounding wildly as she dipped the cup into the sparkling water and lifted it to her mouth. After emptying the cup, a sense of occasion prompted the girl to hold the cup aloft for the view of the surrounding crowd. This action was met by a resounding cheer and the king, with a smile on his face, descended from his throne and made his way towards Rosamund who had risen to her feet. Nodding again at his captain of the guard, the monarch held out his hand to Rosamund and then presented her to the crowd with the words:

'Here is my destined partner — the examiner of men's hearts; the guardian of loyalty!'

Meanwhile, the captain had gone behind the canopy and emerged leading the most magnificent horse Rosamund had ever seen.

'My gift to you, my dear,' said the king, 'to celebrate this momentous occasion.'

The horse was tall — Rosamund thought that it might even be over seventeen hands high. He was unnerved by the circumstances in which he found himself and he reared and plunged in turn, and the captain of the guard found him difficult to control. He was magnificently built and entirely black with a coat that shone with good health. Integrated with the bridle that he wore was a protective head plate of silver that contrasted with his magnificent black coat. Rosamund noted that the saddle was crafted and polished to perfection and that it also had gleaming inserts of decorative silver. Rosamund, with her love and appreciation of beautiful animals, was entirely captivated!

The girl was conscious of the drama of the moment and she knew that she had a role to play. She knew that she should present an image of regal splendour so she resisted the desire to fuss over the animal and simply acknowledged the gift with a slight bow to the king who had let go of her hand and had stepped several paces back. (From this point onwards, Rosamund became aware that the king always physically distanced himself from her — never standing closer than several metres.)

As yet the girl did not know if she had received a gift from the waters of the stream and what indeed that gift might be.

The whole party, including courtiers, soldiers and other witnesses to the afternoon events, retired to the nearby Monastery of The Three Peaks. The main hall had been decorated with banners, and tables were richly set up for the celebratory night's feast. That night during the feast the king, who was sitting in a central position on the main table, passed a written message to Rosamund who was sitting further down the table to his right. The message read: *Rosamund, sleep well tonight, my dear, and tomorrow you will test your newly acquired talent. I want you to meet me in the courtyard of the monastery at ten o'clock and you in your role as my partner can formally review the Royal Guard.* Rosamund was confused and perplexed!

The girl left the banquet soon after and did indeed retire early, but it was many hours before she fell asleep. She was troubled by the nature of what her newly acquired talent might be and why she had been given the task of reviewing the Royal Guard. What troubled her further was that more and more the king used the word *partner* and he now used words like *dear* or *our* and she thought that he might be intending to consolidate their new relationship with marriage.

I do not even like him, thought Rosamund, *but what is to be done?*

The girl rose early and was ready well before the hour of ten o'clock. The soldiers were already standing to attention when the girl and her monarch arrived. At a nod from the king, a sergeant barked the words, 'Present arms!'

When they were at the head of the first rank of men, the king, who had maintained a distance from the girl, said, 'Now, my dear, I want you to pause at each soldier and look into his eyes for a moment or two and concentrate your focus on that man alone. Do not allow any other thought to distract your focus.' It was during the review of the troops that Rosamund discovered her gift — the legacy from the old sorcerer given generations before: Rosamund knew whether a person was truly and completely loyal. She could read people's minds and hearts!

First Skirmishes

The initial skirmish between the king's soldiers and the rebels happened in the first week of spring. The children within the rebel training camp had already set out with two rebel soldiers for the adjoining country of Scarpland and Garth, although exhilarated at the prospect of at last taking on the king's forces, was missing his friend, Naomi, terribly.

He was thinking about the girl as they were making their way along the outskirts of a wood in the lower area of the mountain range. They had reached the edge of a snowdrift left over from the deep winter snows when Juget hissed a warning. The rebels' training kicked directly in. They fell flat to the ground and remained alert and silent. Then they saw what the warrior woman had seen: the flash of the spring sun on weapons.

The soldiers had not seen them, so the guerrillas worked at crawling to positions behind rocks and trees which would allow a situation of ambush. When Juget gave the order to attack the patrol was indeed taken by surprise. After an initial period of confusion, in which they suffered heavy losses, their training also locked in and they were able to offer some reasonable resistance. Still, the ambush had done its damage and the soldiers eventually retreated, in some confusion, into the nearby woods.

It was Garth's first encounter with the horror of battle. Sometimes during training sessions he had wondered how he would react when he took part in his first fight. Would he be overcome with fear? Would he remember his training? Would he be able to hurt another human being?

After watching the soldiers retreat in confusion into the trees he was suddenly overcome by exhaustion. He felt as if all life was draining from him and he was forced to sink to the ground to a sitting position. In a dazed frame of mind, the boy checked himself for any injuries and it was then that he noticed his hands had started to tremble. *At least they were not trembling during the fighting*, he told himself ruefully.

Going over the encounter in his own mind, Garth recalled that although he had been hot with the urgency of battle and that he had not taken a backward step, he had still felt an underlying repugnance at the pain that he had caused a soldier as he had slashed his sword hard into the man's arm. The boy looked around at the twelve or so men that were lying in pain on the ground and he struggled to his feet in order to attend to their wounds. He actually found in a sitting position in the snow the soldier he had defeated in the engagement, cradling his arm. Garth fell to his knees beside the man, tore a section of cloth off his own tunic and bound the soldier's wound.

Perhaps I am not fit for the quest that has been given to me, he told himself. He rose to his feet and saw that Juget was looking at him reflectively.

As always, they were careful not to leave tracks that could give away where they lived in the mountains, so after leaving the scene of their engagement it was some considerable time before they made it back to their monastery camp. Theirs was not the only successful encounter with the king's troops that day; there was one other. These two successful skirmishes gave the rebels considerable encouragement about eventually overcoming the overwhelming odds they faced.

That night saw something of a celebration in the ancient and dilapidated monastery that served as their training camp and headquarters. Garth could not spend too long in celebration because he was heart-sick at the physical pain that he had caused fellow human beings. He also ruminated that his course had been set and that there would be many more such encounters — if indeed he survived to fight them.

He longed to talk to someone about the turmoil that he was experiencing, and in the absence of Naomi he tried to pull aside his friend, the troll. The troll was not feeling any such confusion. In fact, he was intent upon reliving every moment of the military encounter of the early morning by acting out exaggerated details in front of an admiring band of rebels who had been absent from the fray!

The boy left the hall for the refreshing cool air outside, and with a heavy heart slid to the ground, taking comfort from the cold earth. In the end it was Juget who found him outside the hall sitting with his back against the wall of the infirmary and looking up at the stars. The woman touched him gently on the shoulder and passed him a warm comforting drink. She slipped down on the ground beside him and Garth was grateful that she did not try to engage him in conversation, but simply joined him in contemplating the stars.

Victories — Defeat

Many such engagements happened over the succeeding weeks with a significant amount of success for the rebel group. Garth had been in six or seven of these encounters and had received several injuries that were not serious but were nonetheless painful. The boy warrior, however, refused to take time out in the infirmary to recover and always reported for duty the next day. His courageous dedication was exemplary and was noted by all his comrades.

One morning in late spring when the forest was coming into full shiny green leaf, Garth set out with Taymore and a rebel force — including the troll — from a temporary camp they had set up in the foothills of the mountains near where the main route to higher ground began. They had been away from their training base at the old monastery for about a week, using the densely wooded foothills as cover to observe enemy troop movements.

The branches of the tall oaks were spread wide and the green of the birch tree foliage contrasted with the white silvery bark of their trunks. Garth thought how beautiful and different this part of the lower mountains and foothills were, and he allowed himself to imagine how it would be to camp and linger here in autumn when the colours of the leaves would be magnificent. He promised himself that if he lived through these difficult times he would return to see the trees in their autumn splendour.

However, a week of rain along with the residue of melting snow had made the soil underfoot soggy and very slippery. They were moving with a minimum of noise since their scouts had reported seeing a patrol of the king's soldiers in the vicinity late on the previous day.

They heard the noise of the approaching soldiers before they actually saw them. Taymore signalled to the group to take cover behind the surrounding rocks and trees, intimating that he himself would call the order to attack. Garth unsheathed his sword and in so doing was careful to hide the polished metal from the rays of the sun.

Their leader waited till the patrol was almost level with them before he gave his war cry and the rebels sprang into action. Swords flashed in the afternoon sun, and in spite of the ferocious activity, Garth was able to reckon that they were only marginally outnumbered and that the element of surprise had worked significantly in their favour. Taymore had once told him: "The forest with its cover of trees and dense undergrowth suits the type of fighting that we are trained for. Soldiers cannot form charging formations or they do not have time or space to form archery lines".

He was at first challenged by a giant of a man who was wearing light armour. Their swords clashed and Garth felt the man's superior strength, but at the same time it came into his mind what he had been told by a rebel soldier during a training session. Garth had complained to him that in spite of his growth spurt he was still small compared to a fully grown man.

"A large size can be an advantage, of course", the trainer had said, "but it can also be used against a warrior, for it can make him ungainly. A smaller man — if he is smart — can out-think him and use his lesser bulk by being more mobile and getting under his guard".

That is exactly what Garth did now. He ducked down to make his size even smaller and at the same time, drove his sword hard into the man's side in an upward thrust. The soldier screamed with pain but it fleetingly registered with Garth that he did not feel the same compassion for a man's pain as he had in the first skirmish of the campaign.

There is no doubt about it, he told himself, *I have become harder*. It was one of the things that he had feared and worried about on that first night after their initial encounter with the king's soldiers.

Garth withdrew his sword out of the man's side and raised his sword arm, only to bring it down onto the man's shoulder. This brought the warrior down to the ground but Garth did not waste further time on the man.

He engaged another soldier who had materialised to his right.

All around him the fighting raged, but for one second Garth caught sight of the troll swinging from a low branch and meeting with the force of his small but powerful body a soldier who was set to spear a rebel leader who had lost his footing and had fallen to the ground. The rebel leader, known as Robert the Indestructible, saved by the brave and capable action of the troll, regained his balance and continued to take part in the fray.

In many ways the muddy conditions favoured Taymore and his troop, and after only a half an hour or so they had subdued the patrol. Taymore and his men were bloodied and exhausted but they had the soldiers well and truly beaten. Those soldiers that were not lying on the ground were scurrying off into the cover of the trees. The troll was doing a victory dance interspersed with a re-enactment of how he had swung from a low lying branch onto the head of a burley soldier! Several of the rebels, including Taymore and Garth, were attending to the wounded. They did not ignore the injuries of the king's soldiers, giving them equal care.

Later, when he had time to reflect, Garth wondered how it happened without them noticing it. He was bent over attending to a soldier's arm wound when he heard Taymore's exclamation. He looked up and he too let out an explanation of surprise. Encircling them from the undergrowth and trees was a force of about a hundred and fifty armed soldiers, including a line of archers. Coldly observing them (and obviously in charge), seated on a magnificent black war horse was a regal-looking girl of about seventeen years of age.

She was partially dressed in armour. Her silver armour, matching the head plate on her heavy but beautiful war horse, caught the light of the sun shining through the trees. Her clothes were made of the finest light brown leather and finished at their hems with gold and silver fringes. Attached to the pommel of her saddle was a quiver of arrows and in her hand she held a longbow. Two giant, ragged and handsome hounds were either side of her horse, intently waiting for her to give them an order. All this he took in at a glance — and he knew that the girl sitting on the horse was his sister!

Rosamund turned from looking at the group to looking at Garth in particular. Slowly and deliberately she withdrew an arrow from her quiver and placed it in her bow while all the time she coldly held Garth's gaze. She drew back the string, took aim at his right leg and then let the arrow fly.

The pain was excruciating! Garth could not believe the cold and deliberate way the girl had wounded him. He drew in his breath in disbelief as she placed another arrow in her bow and he expected that she would shoot him again — probably in the other leg.

She intends to cripple me! he thought in dismay. This time, however, she looked away from Garth and focused on the troll, and after taking slow and deliberate aim, she let her second arrow fly. Her aim was true. The arrow found its mark and imbedded itself into the side of the troll. The soldiers watched her actions with interest, and like her two hounds, waited for her orders.

She took another arrow from her quiver, still focusing on the troll, and Garth surmised that she intended to finish him off. Garth acted as quickly as his wounded leg would allow. He hurriedly dragged himself over to the prone body of his friend and covered it with his own. Against all his previous intentions, Garth pleaded with an enemy — not for himself but for his brave and loyal friend.

'I beg you, lady, kill me if you must but *please* do no further harm to my friend!' The young woman looked long and hard at Garth, and with a faint smile placed her third arrow back in her quiver.

There had not been a call for an act of surrender — there had been no need, for the odds had been devastatingly overwhelming. At a nod from the young woman, the soldiers had simply moved in and disarmed the rebels and ordered them to move off in the direction that they indicated.

Before moving off, two of the warrior monks snapped the stem of the arrow in Garth's leg and then helped him to his feet. With an arm around each of them, the wounded boy stumbled off. Garth looked over his shoulder at the figure of the troll but he was deathly still. When they reached more open ground the prisoners were chained together and then they were moved off down the mountain. At the base of the mountain range they were met by tumble carts drawn by teams of two horses, and for days they were driven south to the palace of the king.

When they arrived at their destination they were taken down into the dungeons under the palace, unchained and crowded together in a large damp cell with very little light. The same two monks who had broken the shaft of the arrow from Garth's leg finally had an opportunity to set about removing the arrow head itself which was embedded in the calf of his leg.

The monks had no instruments to work with and this did not help in their efforts to relieve the acute pain that the boy warrior was feeling. The physical pain that Garth felt at the removal of the remainder of the arrow was nothing, however, compared to the mental pain of loss that he felt for the absence of his dear and roguish friend, the troll.

A Failed Quest

Sometime in the late hours of that first night in the dungeon of the palace, the jailer, along with four armed guards, stood at the barred entrance to the cell. For some time they looked intently at the inmates and then the jailer pointed at Garth, inserted a key into the lock and opened the door. Two of the soldiers moved into the cell to either side of the boy, and roughly taking an arm each, dragged him out into the corridor. At the jailer's instruction they then dragged him further along down the corridor to another cell door which the jailer opened, and Garth found himself pushed through a doorway that had firstly a thick cast iron door and then directly behind it a barred door. He heard in stunned silence both of the doors being slammed shut and locked behind him.

The rough treatment that he had received did not go well with the wound in his leg and the boy was forced to sit on the bare earth floor so as to take any weight off it. There was no window in the cell and the thick cast iron door prevented any light penetrating his cell from the outside corridor. It took a long time for the ache in his leg to settle enough for him to lie down, and aided by absolute exhaustion, the boy started to nod off to sleep.

His sleep was fitful and troubled. All the way in the tumble cart to the palace, Garth had thought about the quest that had been his legacy from his parents. He reasoned that in spite of his best efforts he had failed. He constantly asked himself, *what more could I have done?* and he concluded that he was simply not up to the task. *I have failed my country and its people; my grandparents and... and... the memory of my parents.*

From time to time he woke from his troubled sleep. The continuous throbbing in his leg led him to suspect that the arrow wound had become infected. At some time — probably in the early hours of the morning — the cast iron door was opened. A figure stood in the entrance and regarded him through the bars of the second door. By this time the fever had really taken a hold and Garth, who was now in a semi-conscious state, was never sure if he had seen a figure looking at him or whether the silent figure had been a figment of his fevered imagination.

Garth had indeed been observed by none other than Rosamund! The boy warrior had aroused her interest. As the king's privileged examiner, she had ordered his removal from the large general cell to the smaller cell for closer observation. She had been told that he was a suspected member of one of the old families — probably he was a distant member of her own family, the Adagio family — and this intrigued her.

Due to her family connection, she wondered if she would feel some regret when he was to be the first of the prisoners to be executed in a staged event in front of the royal court. The king had insisted that she be the one to oversee the whole drama. She thought that her Adagio family background was the reason the king wanted her to manage his execution when he had said to her:

'This young rebel is a great danger to the stability of our country, Rosamund. He is cruel and unscrupulous and he will stop at nothing to topple us. It would be good if you were the one to supervise the sentence of death.'

'Would you like me to read his mind — look into his heart?' the girl had asked.

'No, no!' he had replied with emphasis. 'There is no need. Nothing would be gained by so doing.' So Rosamund, ever keen to prove herself a dedicated and faithful partner of the king, set about arranging the dramatic events that were to surround Garth's punishment.

About mid-morning on the fourth day of the rebel's imprisonment in the dungeon, an armed patrol came to fetch Garth and take him up to the great hall of the king's palace. By then, the infection in his leg had mercifully died down and the pain was not as intense. Still, it was very sore and the way the soldiers dragged him along did not improve its condition. His discomfort was further heightened by the fact that he had been given little to eat or drink over the past few days and his clothes were torn and bloodied.

Their *Parents' Bequest*

*I*t was some distance from the dungeon to the main body of the castle where the king had his throne room or, more accurately, throne hall. On leaving his cell Garth had to concentrate on staying on his feet as the squad of soldiers who surrounded him (including two ceremonial drummers) marched at a quick pace. He tried to linger at the door of the large general cell where his friends were held. He felt the need to see them once again before what, he reasoned, was to be his ordeal of execution. The soldiers, however, did not allow him to slow down his steps and he was roughly pushed forward.

Garth did see his friends rush to the barred door and he did hear words of encouragement coming from the cell. He particularly heard the voice of Taymore say to him the words that were inscribed at the base of the pendant which he still wore around his neck, and which the boy had previously shared with the rebel leader: 'Courage is crafted in adversity.'

The words did indeed encourage Garth and he became determined, come what may, to be courageous to the end.

When they entered the main corridor leading to the throne hall Garth, in spite of his bravery, felt most dreadfully alone. The buzz of voices that issued from the hall told him that his execution was to be witnessed by a large crowd — probably the king and his court. He fervently wished that he could have a friend to focus on before and during his ordeal.

The crowd within the hall were alerted to the approach of Garth and his guard by the dramatic beating of the ceremonial drums, and the buzz of voices ceased. The long and imposing hall was decorated with rich tapestries of hunting scenes featuring the king himself as the lead person in the hunt.

Pivotal to the scene in the throne hall was the prominent position of the king in full ceremonial robes, sitting on his highly ornate throne. Garth's eyes, however, were drawn away from the spectacle of the king to the image of the sinister block of wood and the masked executioner holding an axe. In spite of his intense feelings of aloneness on entering the hall, the scene before him did not rob the boy of his determination to be courageous. This determination was further supported by a deep sense of peace which had entered his spirit on hearing the words of Taymore.

What did rob him of some peace, however, was the sight of the composure of the girl sitting on her own separate dais not ten metres from the executioner. Apparently there was to be little delay and the girl, in a controlled voice, rose up on her dais and read the charges against the boy warrior. He was condemned, she said, because of his rebellious actions against the lawful ruler of their land and for his encouragement of others to also rise up in rebellion.

'All take note,' she said in a solemn voice, 'that those who follow this course of action will be subject to the same punishment.' Then she turned to the masked executioner and gave an order.

Garth's emotions rushed to the surface and he could not contain himself.

'You order my death without knowing who I am and why I have sought you out. Why is it so easy to order my death? You are like your cruel master — you leave all your evil deeds to others!'

'Not so,' said the young woman. 'I am the king's examiner and you are lucky that your death will be swift and that you are not being interrogated!' Garth could not believe his ears.

'My own sister is the king's examiner!' he muttered to himself in a low agonised tone.

'Witness this death!' she said to the surrounding court. 'This youth is a member of the Adagio family — my *own* family. I give up my family to be a loyal follower of our king, the rightful ruler of Balkonia!'

There was a sinister smile of approval on the king's face as he watched the drama unfold before him.

'It has worked,' he said under his breath. 'The girl will cement my rule! She is a triumph!' He regarded her magnificent and awesome image, and he thought again of what had occupied him much of late: that she indeed would make him a fitting wife (if only he could allow her to see into his heart and mind!).

Garth's courage, nurtured from the early days by his grandparents, had increased enormously by drinking at The Crystal Stream, and his dedicated training with the rebels did not desert him now! He felt a deep and frustrating anger… he had travelled so far! He had been through so much to find, and rescue, his sister but she was not to be saved! She was willingly in the service of a repressive and evil king. The peace he had felt at hearing Taymore's parting words had entirely left him. He thought again, with agonised regret, how he had failed. His grandparents would suffer yet another family loss and he would not be there to help them survive through their remaining years.

Trembling with fury, he roared at the young woman who was only a short distance from him and he expressed the only defiance that was open to him.

'Why do you have others do your cruel work? Have the courage to kill me yourself!'

Rosamund stood in regal silence. From a scabbard deep in the folds of her long royal blue velvet robe which fell in folds to her feet, she drew a long glistening sword.

'As you wish,' said the girl. Her raven black hair was drawn back, set with multiple braids and tied with gold ribbons. Garth, in spite of his anger and deadly situation, thought that he had never seen anyone so awesome and splendid.

In response to his challenge she walked slowly down the stairs from the raised dais. All the while her gaze never left him. Everyone in the hall was drawn to the mesmerising sight. The expression on the dark monarch's face did not betray his absolute glee.

This is beyond all expectation, he said to himself. *The girl is going to kill her brother herself!* As she neared Garth she raised her sword hand high and the boy, sick with anticipation, mentally prepared himself to receive a death stroke from the fall of her sword. It achingly flashed through his whole being that Rosamund would never know that she had dealt the death blow to her only brother.

It should have been so different! he told himself. *We should have lived in friendship and affection.*

Due to his closed eyes Garth did not see her hand stop its fall. With the sword still poised, Rosamund looked with amazement at the pendant that Garth wore around his neck. The boy opened his eyes, however, when he heard her say aloud the words, 'Courage is crafted in adversity.' There was a short silence as the girl felt for the pendant around her own neck, and having found it, demanded in an imperious voice:

'Where did you get your pendant from?'

He could not answer immediately because of the trauma that had overtaken his whole system. After swallowing hard he answered in as clear and strong a voice as he could muster.

'It belongs to my family. *Your* family — *our* family! Our mother left it to me just before she was killed by the king that you serve so slavishly! Our grandmother placed it around my neck as I set out on my journey to find you, my sister, and…' He stopped himself from completing the sentence which would have been a statement of his intent to rid the country of their cruel and ruthless king.

Rosamund stood in stunned silence. She achieved then what she had tried to achieve on the night when she had regarded Garth from his cell door. She had eye contact with the young man and she was close enough to read his mind and judge his heart. Her gift passed down from the sorcerer all those years ago encountered the gift that her brother had received from the same wise old man. She came face to face with enormous dedicated courage, and she was overwhelmed by its beauty.

After a short interval the girl said silently to herself, *My brother! My brother! The king has nearly tricked me into killing my own brother*! The time that she spent helplessly standing before Garth was enough for her to remember so much: the poverty of the people that she had seen in the marketplace, and the old lady in the same marketplace who had pleaded with her to combine with her brother to restore the land. She remembered the disappearance of both her fitness instructor and the supposed accidental death of her old hunting master. Even the treatment of Petra now aroused some sense of pity. She became acutely aware of her seclusion in both her own castle and the king's palace and her lack of contact with the outside world.

Oh, why was I so easily taken in? she said to herself. *Why did I believe his lies so easily? Why did I not question the way things were? I have been nothing more than a puppet in recent times, exposing to his cruelty those who have challenged — if only in their minds — his right to rule! I have been seduced by the luxury in which I live and by the enjoyment of exercising power over others.*

She felt helpless with the waste of it all, but it was not in her nature or training to allow the helplessness to last. The coldness and hardness that the king had so nurtured in her took over, and she quickly formed in her mind a course of action.

She took her eyes off the courageous image of her younger brother and turned instead to the image of the king sitting on his throne. She re-sheathed her sword, and walking towards the dark monarch with a faint and disarming smile, said, 'Before we proceed further, may I have a word with you, sire?'

The king, like everyone else in the hall, was confused. He, unlike Rosamund, could not read minds, so the troubled state of the young woman and the flashes of truth that she had experienced in the minutes before were unknown to him, so too the course of revengeful action that she had determined upon.

The girl mounted the steps to the king's throne and the monarch leant forward to better hear what Rosamund was going to say to him. The girl, without hesitation, flicked the crown from his head and grabbed his hair. At the same time, she unsheathed her sword, and with a movement that was quick and certain, severed his head.

Blood gushed from the headless trunk which Rosamund pulled from the throne and thrust down the stair to the floor below; the head, she held aloft for the courtiers and soldiers to see. She seemed impervious to the blood which dripped from the dark monarch's dead head onto her arms and clothes, but she was aware of the shocked and stunned silence of the court that surrounded her and she knew that every moment that followed was critical.

The king lay dead in a pool of blood. His head had at last been thrown disdainfully by Rosamund onto the floor of the throne room and it lay at an obscene distance from the truncated body. Rosamund had been trained to hardness, and in recent times, to power, and by the king's own proclamation had been made second only to himself in the land.

The girl looked steadily around the room. She seemed to each member of the court, including the royal guard, to be able to see into their minds, and they trembled in her presence. She took advantage of the shock effect of her having ruthlessly decapitated the king moments before, and she knew that any action would be supported by her awesome presence. In theatrical splendour, she grasped the moment. The girl knew exactly what to do in order to organise things so that her power was established and possibilities of resistance among soldiers and courtiers were negated.

Down in the dungeons the rebel prisoners waited sadly all day to hear of Garth's fate. They waited also with bravery and resolve to face their own reckoning with the king which they imagined would be cruel and without mercy.

Rosamund knew that the blood-stained clothes she continued to wear added greatly to the dramatic effect of her takeover and she made no attempt to change them during the course of the day. Near enough to midnight that night there was turmoil in the corridors as a blood-stained and imperious Rosamund entered the dungeons with her brother by her side. It had occurred to her that there might be considerable value in using the rebels imprisoned in the dungeon to gain further support for her position.

The vision of Garth's dedicated courage — his purity of purpose had not only awed Rosamund but had worked a certain subtle magic. She was not immediately converted to other values but the process had begun. If truth be told, while she had enjoyed the power that the king had given her, she had never really wanted total power over the kingdom. On beheading the king, however, common sense dictated that she had to assume power and a persona of ruthlessness. Hesitation to do so would have seen ambitious elements in the court step up to destroy her and the boy, who was her newly discovered brother.

When a person is associated with selfishness, arrogance and evil there is a risk of contamination. Things can also work in reverse: association with unselfishness and goodness can have positive effects, too. Time with her brother and his dedicated and good companions gradually took effect on Rosamund. The girl was won over to the possibility that the country could best be governed in the ancient and just ways of past times, and this is what she came to work for.

The time that Rosamund spent with her brother did not remove a certain reserve that existed between them, however. Garth found it difficult to talk to his sister in spite of her efforts to be courteous toward him. Although it had lessened considerably, Rosamund still had an air of inapproachability, and her brother held her in awe. Along with this awe, deep down in his heart there were still elements of resentment and anger because his sister had abused the old sorcerer's gift by accepting the role of examiner. On the other hand, the girl tried desperately not to allow her gift of discernment to intrude into her day-to-day relationships (particularly with her brother and the inner core of the rebel group), yet she knew that there was much to repair before total trust could be established.

She felt a need to propel this time forward and a need to formally acknowledge the self-sacrifice of the rebel group and the efforts of her brother, in particular. In consultation with some members of the old families, Rosamund determined that the leaders of the rebels should be subject to the ancient right of knighthood.

One glorious day just after dawn a group of people, including Rosamund, rode out from the palace grounds to a clearing deep in the forest where those chosen for knighthood had been left a week before to spend time in thought and meditation. The forest was dressed in full summer splendour and the shiny greenwood trees, along with the vibrant birdsong, acted as a perfect backdrop for a ceremony which granted knighthood status to Taymore, Juget and seven others, including Garth. Over the preceding weeks, Rosamund had given much thought to the titles that the knights should receive. For her brother she chose the title: Garth the Courageous.

The Forming of a Just Government

Rosamund formed a council so as to deliberate how the country might best be nurtured into prosperity. She selected wise people to be part of the council: three members of the old court remained but mostly she selected councillors from the rebels' group. In time, and as her own good intentions crafted her into a better and wiser person, Rosamund removed herself from control of the council and started to take a less prominent role. Before doing so, she appointed the old monk, Francis, to take her place as leader of the group. Francis was a humble man and he did not want to accept the role. Brother Oliver, who was his long-time companion, placed his hand on Francis's shoulder.

'Take the role — for a time. Help us formulate a just and good constitution which will give us long-term direction. Then you can retire to your books, my dear old friend.'

The council was determined not to waste any opportunity to instigate just rule, and as they discussed a possible constitution, they noticed that Francis, although chairperson, rarely spoke.

'What are your ideas, Brother Francis? You hardly ever speak. Are we heading in the right direction?' asked Juget who had been wisely chosen by Rosamund to be a member of the council.

Brother Francis thought for a moment before speaking. 'You are doing your best to bring about a just order modelled on the past. But what we have is an opportunity to bring in something new. Why must it be the old families that rule? Why could we not create a council just like ours but peopled by representatives from all levels of society so that every area would have a chance to have their interests heard?' Here Francis paused so that what he had said could be mulled over by those present, and then after several minutes he continued.

'Those chosen would have to be wise people, and if at any time they started to put their own interests above those of the people they should serve, they would be replaced by new representatives. What do you think? It would mean, of course, that we ourselves would have to retire from governorship so as to give an example of interest and unselfishness.'

At first there was incredulity because even among just people there is a tendency to hold on to power, but after much discussion the councillors started to see the wisdom of Francis's plan for the future and they tentatively worked towards establishing such a council.

The ideas put forward by the monk resonated with Garth and he set to thinking where he had heard similar ideas before.

Plato's The Republic — *that was it*! he told himself one day. His grandparents had read it to him over several evenings in what seemed a long time ago. Francis was adapting the ideas of Plato to suit their particular purposes, and he thought that his sister had made an excellent choice when choosing Francis to direct them.

Rosamund had recognised the goodness and wisdom of the old monk and each day she would meet with him in the garden of the dead king's palace to talk with him about her past and how she might progress into spiritual goodness.

'A good start would be to relinquish the gift of reading hearts and intentions,' said the old monk, 'for therein lies your sense of power, and if you strive for humility you must divest yourself of the love of power.'

'How can I do that?'

'Practise humility whenever you can and then re-drink the waters of The Crystal Stream. The stream may gift you again by removing this power,' said the old man, all the time looking into the girl's eyes to gauge her reaction.

It took Rosamund sometime before she arrived at a mental and spiritual state where she could travel to the Monastery of the Three Peaks to hopefully divest herself of her strange power. In time she did, and the stream did gift her again by removing the power that it had once given. With her relinquishment of power came a desire to return to her origins and meet her grandparents.

Garth also desperately wanted to return to visit his grandparents. He knew that by now they would be aware of what had happened over the past several months: the removal of the king and the establishment of a council. Indeed, the benefits of these changes were already filtering down to the general population. Rosamund brought up the subject one day at the conclusion of a meeting of the council. Brother and sister then determined on a date for departure.

A Journey Towards Peace and Reconciliation

In the spirit of her search for simplicity and peace, the caravan that Rosamund chose to accompany her to meet her grandparents was simple and without pretentions. Garth, a few members of the council, her two faithful deer hounds, and a doctor to tend to the sick troll (and the troll himself), were all that set out on the journey to the river.

The boy, faithful to the promise that he had made to the troll months before — that there would always be a place at his fireside for him — would not leave his wounded friend behind. They left early one morning from the palace on the central plains and travelled east till they came to the river along which Garth had travelled in reverse at the outset of his quest. From there, they meandered along the river's course, camping each night along its bank.

To the surprise of everyone, Rosamund did not find the privations of the journey so trying. On the contrary, she took them in her stride. The girl was probably aided in this by the basic nature of the hunting trips that she had taken with the old hunting master, Leopold, which she had found so pleasurable.

Garth spent as much time as he could with the injured troll. The poor little fellow. After being wounded, he had been left by the soldiers to die in the forest. On the day after the king had been deposed, a party had hurriedly left the palace to find and retrieve him, if indeed he was still alive. They found the troll in a serious state, but by virtue of great care he was kept alive.

During the long hours of the day Garth would walk beside the troll's stretcher. He made it his duty to call a halt to their journey at least every two hours so that he could put cool water to the lips of his semi-conscious friend and rest him from the continual jolting of the stretcher. On one such break during their trek, Garth looked long and hard at the troll and spoke his thoughts aloud.

'All this time that we have been together you have never told me your name. Indeed, I have never asked you. I have always just called you Troll.'

To his surprise the troll partly opened his eyes and said in a faltering voice:

'I do not yet have a personal name. It is not our way to name the young. All trolls are called Trillius at birth and then, over time, another name is given according to how he or she acts as their life goes on.'

After speaking these words the troll lapsed back into semi-consciousness. Garth looked at the prone figure for a long time and then said to him:

'My friend, from now on you shall be called Trillius the Brave.' The troll briefly opened his great luminous eyes and smiled at his friend, Garth.

On the third night of their journey they camped as they had the night before by the banks of the river, and after the evening meal, Garth set out for a quiet stroll before retiring for the night.

The boy wandered along the river bank until he came near to where Trillius the Brave had been placed upon a stretcher in one of the few tents that had been erected by the travelling party. At a distance Garth was surprised to see the kneeling figure of his sister. She was bathing the wound by the light of a small lamp that her arrow had made in the troll's side. One of the monks had proclaimed that the little fellow had made it through the worst of the effects of the wound but he was still falling in and out of consciousness.

The lad held back from approaching the tent out of a certain awe at the beauty of the situation. His regal sister, who had only known the role of being served, was finishing the dressing to the wound. Then she tenderly lifted the shaggy head of the troll and held it while he accepted a drink from an earthen bowl.

After her ministrations, the girl slowly walked from the tent, and it was then that her brother intercepted her.

'Walk a little way with me?' he said quietly. They walked for some distance but all the while Rosamund's head was bowed. At last Garth stepped forward and stood so that his sister's eyes could not be averted from his own. He saw confusion and guilt spread across her face and she raised her hands in a gesture of helplessness. Then she let them fall to her sides.

'We should walk always and talk together,' said Garth. They left the bank of the river and followed a path that led them to higher ground. Rosamund broke the silence first.

'I am not a good person,' she said slowly. 'For years I have only had myself to please and think of, and in recent times my selfishness and arrogance have known no bounds. I have been in the service of a bad ruler and because it suited me I did not question what I was told.' Then her face clouded over and Garth knew she was remembering wasted and untruthful years. 'Before very recent times I allowed myself to desire more and more power, and Garth, the greatest corrupter of the human spirit is a love of power.

'And... then there have even been times when I enjoyed seeing fear in someone's eyes. With power came a certain... hardness... an insensitivity, and I do not know how I can work backwards and regain what I surely must have had once.' For a while there was silence and Garth said:

'You have more than started your journey back, Rosamund. Continue the course you have now set and all will be well.' For a moment or two Garth lost the awe that he felt for his sister, and he felt that *he* was the older sibling.

The girl then said to her brother, 'How will it work? After what I have done, how can I be accepted by the people — even our grandparents?'

Touched by her pain and uncertainty, Garth hesitatingly stretched out his hand and touched her gently on the shoulder.

'You were a victim, too, like our parents. Indeed, just like all the people of this poor land. And...' here the boy struggled for words, 'our grandparents will welcome you — just you wait and see. Remember they nursed you as a baby and they have mourned your loss all these years. You might even remember something about them when you see them again. Although you do not realise it, you know much about how things stand in the country. Your advice and co-operation with the council you have established will be of invaluable service to council members as they seek to develop a just system of government.'

After another long pause Rosamund said, 'Should we send for horses and ride the rest of the way?'

'No, I believe there is much value in continuing as we started. We should walk and that will give us time to talk about things to come and... time to talk about things that have passed.'

The girl then averted her eyes from her brother as she said with obvious shame, 'What about the wound in your leg?'

'Please do not think about that. It is healing well and so long as we walk at a reasonable pace it will be fine.'

The smell of wood smoke, along with the notes of music, drifted up to them from the campfire further down on the bank of the river and Garth realised that someone was singing along to the slow strumming of the lute. The song was not a robust early evening song but a mellow lilting melody that belonged to the late hours of the night. Garth thought that the song probably told of sorrow, pain or loss.

The brother and sister sat quietly, straining to hear the words that were just beyond hearing. It was a clear night and there was a new moon and the stars were out in abundant splendour in a deep purple sky. The music made him think of Naomi and how he missed her, and how he desperately wanted to go and fetch her and the other young people back from exile. He knew there were some things that had to be done before he saw her again and that others would bring her back.

But we will eventually be together, my soulmate and I! thought Garth, with an intensity of feeling that surprised him.

When the song finished Garth noted that Rosamund had bowed her head forward again and he found a need to comfort her. From deep in his memory he drew the words that his grandmother had said to him all those months ago as he set out on his long quest. He pulled the pendant from underneath his tunic, and after examining it for some time, said to his sister:

'I think we have both been crafted through adversity and eventually we have both made it through.' Rosamund raised her head and both brother and sister looked intently into each other's eyes. Any remainder of resentment that the boy may have had at the core of his being towards his sister melted away, and brother and sister were at last finally and completely reconciled in hope of a deep friendship in the future.